SMOKE SHADOWS

PAMELA ST ABBS

ISBN: 957403046
ISBN-13: 9780957403048
First published as an e-book

DEDICATION

Bill, Edward and Rosalind

# CONTENTS

# ACKNOWLEDGMENTS

Chris, Gina – now sadly departed – and Maggie for listening to the early drafts of this book and for their support.

# Chapter 1

Catherine flicked on the head lights and turned the ignition key. Robert had said that this was the wrong way to start the car. He had always told her the engine should be fired up, that was his phrase, first. But, perhaps, that was why she did it.

Nevertheless, the car made a rough throbbing noise from under the bonnet, and Catherine reversed around Evelyn and George. Within moments her mother and her mother's friend were lost in dusk as she headed towards home. The radio free journey took fifteen minutes to change from half-light to complete darkness.

It must have been the effort of concentrating on the road which made her head buzz. She was sure it was only her worries for her mother which added to the fuzziness around her eyes.

There was something wrong with Evelyn. There had been more than the usual tension between them. Her mother had given her life and in some peculiar way she had always seemed able to drain her heart and strength from her. But today Evelyn had been remote. She had felt shut out.

The man-made forest started to flick by close to her. It was arranged in neat squares – an orderliness, Catherine decided, nature would not understand. The darkness beyond her headlights seemed unnatural too.

She could smell something. She wasn't sure at first what it was. Slowly it came to her that it was the sort of smell she associated with having a cold. It was then that she started to panic. She knew her body could not tolerate this substance. That had been the reason for her giddiness, not her mother and the night driving. Yet there was nowhere to pull off the road. She was already between the solidity of the forest on one side of the road and a row of poplar trees on the other. They oppressed her. It was as if smoke were

1

filling her lungs, but there was no smoke. She began gasping for breath, but nothing would make her stop in this lonely place. She tried to open the side window, but it wouldn't budge.

The autumn air had turned into a wind and the trees seemed to be stooped towards the road. The car was slowing, out of her control. Catherine looked in disbelief at the dials. The petrol gauge was empty. She coasted the car across the road into the wrong lane and pulled onto the grass verge by the forest. The car stopped.

'You can't do this to me.' She thumped her hands on the steering wheel. The moon flickered between the clouds. She left her headlights on despite the dead engine. 'Damn the battery,' she muttered. She pushed the switch for the internal light. It failed to come on. She pushed it with her clenched fist. Nothing happened. She knew there would be a can of petrol in the boot of the car; there always was. She knew she had to get out of the security of the car to get it. She knew she didn't want to. She waited fifteen minutes in the car, the glow from the digital clock her only comfort. With each minute the wooziness increased until she felt she would pass out.

She swung out into the night air, her loose dark blonde hair caught in the wind and flicked across her face. Her giddiness cleared slightly in the fresh air and she felt along the back of the car for the catch. It gave under her fingers and the boot lid lifted.

Darkness met darkness. The expected courtesy light failed to come on. She couldn't see. She put her hand in and felt around the space. There was nothing in it: no wheel-jack, no tow rope, no torch and no can of petrol. Even the space for the spare wheel was vacant. Catherine rocked back on her heels. The desire to scream was countered with the desire to be invisible, unseen by pervaders of the night. Her conscious will made her stand firm.

In the fresh air she remembered her mobile phone in her pocket. One of her pockets. She fumbled for it. Finding it she tried to phone her husband but the screen kept telling her there was no signal. She tried Sadie: no signal. She tried her mother: no signal. She tried George: no signal. And the thing bleeped and turned itself off: battery dead.

Somewhere she heard a noise. Was it in her head? No, it was a voice. It was distorted in her head. It sounded hollow and screaming. She looked up the road. A shadow was moving. It hovered and swayed changing the density of the other shadows as it passed them. Her vision was distorted inside her brain as was sound. The shadows looked enlarged and solid.

While the wind in the black poplars on the other side of the road away from the forest sounded like a violent sea crashing on the beach. She looked towards the forest. Panic spread through her limbs. She knew she must run. The solid shadow was moving towards her.

Her heart sank as her limbs barely co-operated. Catherine glanced at the forest next to her. A light came on in its depths. It was firm and bright. Her brain was talking to her as if detached from her body. It was telling her to go to it. She received its message, 'You'll be safe here.' Catherine stumbled along the road for a moment looking for a path through to the beckoning light.

The distorted shadow was coming towards her too quickly to be on foot. Catherine screamed. It was a choked involuntary rush of air that was nearly lost by the time it came out of her mouth. Before her mind could sort out the various confusing stimuli, her thin jacket was tearing on this year's growth of brambles. The briers reached across the narrow forest path. She pushed on. Her instinct to survive was more than an isolated desire for her own life. It was the primary requirement of a mother to protect her young.

Somehow she was moving faster now; all giddiness and fuzziness had gone. Her vision seemed acutely aware of her surroundings and her ears heard every crackle of the undergrowth. The voice behind her had stopped but the sounds from its body crashing through the brambles followed her. Her eyes searched out the light. As she approached it disappeared more frequently -- the trees were hiding it with their bulk.

She stopped. The flashlight shone its safe beacon at her from its bed of pine needles. She picked it up. It was sticky but she hung onto it. She could move faster than her pursuer now she had a light. She could hear the voice behind her. It was familiar to her cleared senses. She sighed and stood up. A shudder of relief seemed to leave her flesh loose. She turned the torch in a complete circle taking the beam from pointing towards the road, through the direction she had been going and back towards the voice. All she saw were the trees closest to her. The light beam made them seem unreal, like stage scenery. She couldn't see her pursuer. Had he fallen among the brambles? Her hand stopped and returned the light to the direction she'd just come from.

Catherine dropped the light and screamed. The screams came from the depth of her body and were pushed out with every breath. They weaved through the trees to the sky. Her eyes were closed against the vision before her, but it was too late. In a moment every detail had been imprinted on her mind. With her eyes shut she could still see an iron bar bolted between two pine trees – from it hung a pulley. Attached to the pulley was a blue rope. One end of the blue rope was secured around a cleat fixed into one of the supporting pine trees. The other end was entwined around the feet of a man. He hung upside down with his head just clearing the ground. His trousers curled up to his calves. His jacket sagged about his chest. His arms hung down where his head should have been. His neck was cut through to the spine, but his heart seemed unaware of this fact and was still trying to pump blood into his head. The veil of blood and the angle of the head made the corpse unrecognisable.

Her body buckled forwards while her gut twisted inside.

The familiar voice that had been calling her, pursuing her was suddenly behind her. She heard it as she gasped for breath. In her terror it failed to give her reassurance. All she could do was link it with the horror before her. She didn't want to live. She sank onto the pine needles, prayed, and waited for death.

# Chapter 2

A swarthy man of well over average height, whose body and posture reminded WPC Jenner of an oversized squirrel, stood by a pine tree rubbing his left ear with his left hand. She hadn't met Inspector Campbell before, but she'd heard about him along the gossip tracks of the area's local police stations. She noted his bright nut brown eyes blinking in the glare of the spot-lamps highlighting the scene of the crime.

Along with everyone else, WPC Jenner waited for the question she could not answer. He would be sure to ask it. Numerous possible answers to these unasked questions rushed through her mind. Worse still, she knew he could start talking about the weather or his children's school activities. He would seem unaware of the devastation around him. He would appear to have no thoughts other than those that were written on the notes brought to him as peace offerings by his staff. She wondered if it was being Scottish that made him unpredictable.

'Excuse me, Sir,' said a uniformed man as he twined coloured plastic ribbon around the trees. It made a gaudy trail through the forest, and in its centre the gory remains of a man were being zipped into a body bag. The tall man moved just enough to let the trail proceed.

'Inspector? Inspector Campbell?' WPC Jenner asked him. When he turned she said, 'The woman and her husband, Mr and Mrs Fenman, have been taken to hospital. The couple who found the body?'

'Do you know, I think I've hurt my toe,' said her superior as he wriggled his foot with enthusiasm.

'WPC Garden has gone with them, Sir.'

'Who are you?' he asked, his soft Scottish accent emphasising the first and last words as he moved over to look at the black covered corpse.

Jenner followed. 'WPC Jenner, Sir,' she said.

Inspector Campbell watched the body taken away. It seemed to him that it was going to an even less dignified resting place. The pathologist had remarked at the curious way the body had been hung. It was similar to a slaughtered pig, he'd said. The throat had been cut through to the spine, allowing the head to lie with its face looking backwards. It looked like the work of a butcher. The corpse had been initially identified by one of those bright young constables as Frederick Twilling, the developer. The constable had delighted in telling his audience that this man of means somehow had managed to get his name in the paper every week and his face in it at least once a month. He had smiled until he had been reminded by a watchful sergeant that the man was dead.

A robust middle aged woman straightened. Mary Brown's square-ness always gave Campbell a feeling of security. Her serious expression broke into a warm motherly smile.

'I know you've seen it. I've seen it too. And I know, you know, we've seen it. We've taken photographs and we'll be taking a cast in a moment. No, on second thoughts, Campbell, we'll do it now.' She moved across to a track made in the earth.

Campbell was used to Mary Brown addressing him minus his title. He knew it was the way she addressed everyone: surname only whether male, female, Lord, Lady or Superintendent. It was never an insult; it was her way of making everyone equal. It seemed to him that Mary Brown thought of people as consisting of so many pieces of evidence gathered together in a moving mass. Their only interest being the trail such moving masses of information might leave behind.

'We've found other tyre marks through the forest. We've photographed and taken impressions of those already. There was a foot print too. It was a female shoe so it could have been from the woman that found the body. The tyre tracks lead to a lane on the far side of this section of forest. It's firm gravel so there are no marks, but I've got another team working over there. We will, of course be checking that the wheel tracks were made by the same wheel.'

'What sort of vehicle was it?'

'I can't tell at the moment. The tyre print is eighty five millimetres across. The tread pattern is simple, not the sort you find on a road vehicle, could possibly be a trailer, but we only have one at the moment. You've seen it for yourself.'

Campbell grunted. He knew there had been no mention of the murderer having a car, but he wanted to tease Mary Brown about the efficiency of the forensic investigations, so he said, 'No. I meant the car.'

'What car?' asked Mary.

'The car that brought the murderer and/or the victim here,' explained Campbell.

'We have found no evidence of any car as yet. We will be able to see better in daylight, but that back lane is coarse dark gravel. There are no definite marks on it. We haven't found any flakes of paint yet. If we do we will look into it.' Mary started to spread her chest and snort slightly.

Campbell's face barely flickered with satisfaction at her aggravation. Forensic evidence had changed the detection game. Eyes and ears seemed to have been replaced by microscopes and plastic bags. He'd long since ceased to be amazed that a few drops of genetic material could tell them so much. But he knew it wasn't as easy as that. The mobility of the nation's population meant a forever moving criminal element were able to remain anonymous.

Morning broke through the trees. As natural light became brighter the powerful lamps were turned off.

All that could be gained by a detective with ordinary vision had been observed by Campbell. He tried to assess whether Frederick Twilling would be the murderer's only victim. To be strung up and slaughtered in this way showed hate, or madness, or both. Could someone this mad and this hateful restrict themselves to just one murder? He doubted it. The thought chilled him. He had to make sure it didn't happen again.

Beyond the plastic ribbon people had started to gather despite the efforts of the uniformed police to move them on. He wondered what brought people out to see. Was it simple curiosity, or a morbid desire to glimpse a dead person? Perhaps, such a glimpse would remind them that they were alive. Could it even be a desire to play detective themselves, solve the mystery? He didn't know and suddenly he stopped caring. A bright young thing was gathering speed towards him. He recognised this one. Only the face, the name was a mystery, such things weren't important.

'Inspector. Parnold, Sir.' The arrival introduced himself without prompting.

Campbell grunted in reply.

'We've traced Mrs Sarah Twilling.' The bright young thing looked tired but willing; the horse that would go any distance. The fleshy face of youth was surrounded by soft fair curls. With a splatter of make-up his maleness could have been questioned but his voice was strong with an underlying native Norfolk lilt.

Campbell followed the young man to the car and was driven by him to the widow's home.

The long winding drive gave way to a circle of tarmac in front of sweeping steps leading to closed heavy doors. The curtains were drawn against the world which was so distant Mrs Sarah Twilling wouldn't have been able to see it anyway.

Campbell looked at the woman who answered the gothic toll of the doorbell. She was neither servant nor relative. It was Mrs Sarah Twilling. She was a small slim woman in a chocolate brown suit. Her face was in conflict with itself. There was a sharpness in her nose and chin, yet a softness in her eyes and an innocence in her bearing which made her look as if she'd never seen cruelty. Her amber tinted, once dark hair was un-brushed and her green eyes were tired. Mrs Twilling looked at the uniformed policewoman, whom Parnold had brought along, and the official faces; and lost her strength.

The policewoman helped the woman through to what Mrs Twilling described as the drawing room. Parnold opened the curtains. The room's four tall windows allowed the morning light to cut bright shapes out on the carpet. The pink carpet looked almost white in the overpowering light and the flowered curtains were purpled in the sharp shadow. Mrs Sarah Twilling and the policewoman stood in one of the pools of light. The silhouette took a seat at Campbell's bidding. In the softer light away from the windows she blended with the chintz upholstery. Her outline was soft, her arms and legs were rounded but not fat. Her joints were so supple she matched the curve of the settee completely. The relaxed pose was only a matter of habit though. Campbell saw her eyes had gained the look of a rabbit caught in the headlights of a car.

Campbell's words of explanation for their visit were given with sorrow and sympathy. The woman did not cry; she choked.

'You are dressed early, Mrs Twilling?' asked Parnold. Campbell frowned, but waited for the answer.

'I've not been to bed, I've been up all night worrying,' answered Mrs Twilling. 'It seems strange that now the worst thing that could happen has happened, I don't know what to do.' She choked again and a sob came too. 'We've just moved here,' she explained to anybody, as if such unimportant conversation would keep her exploding emotions at bay. 'And he's been very kind to me.' She gasped at the air and tried to explain, 'I'd been left with nothing. My first husband had run his own business. It'd been successful for a while, but he'd drunk and gambled all the money away. He stumbled across the railway crossing one night and straight into a train. He left me bankrupt. Frederick's been very kind. I don't think either of us wanted the romantic kind of love.' Tears came steadily down her cheek now.

'He sounds as if he was more of a brother than a husband, Mrs Twilling?' Campbell asked once he'd found himself a deep soft chair opposite the settee which contained Mrs Twilling.

'I think he wanted emotional security and I wanted physical security. In that way we needed each other.' Mrs Twilling continued unprompted, 'His first wife had been extremely odd. She'd been in and out of mental institutions all their married life. It left my husband and, particularly, his son, Jonathan, very uptight. The sort of illness she had can be inherited.'

Campbell left the words hanging as she'd said them, a tempting morsel which he would not give her the satisfaction of acknowledging. Instead he asked her an open question, 'What happened yesterday evening, Mrs Twilling?' He knew that if he did not ask her now her memories would soon be tarnished by grief or, perhaps, some less worthy emotion such as greed.

'He left here on foot at about six o'clock. He said he wanted a walk before dinner. I offered to go with him. I said we could eat out – then I wouldn't have to stay and worry about the food. But he wanted to go alone.'

'Was there something wrong?' asked Campbell.

'Not until he wanted to go for this silly walk, there wasn't. I thought I'd done something wrong and he wouldn't talk to me. At the time I was hurt. I didn't want him to leave me here on my own. I watched him walk down the drive.' Her voice broke at the realisation that she would not see him again.

'Mrs Twilling, where does Jonathan Twilling live?' Parnold asked.

'He has the gate house at the bottom of the drive,' she replied.

'Is it possible your husband went to see him last evening?' asked Campbell.

'No, Jonathan phoned about nine o'clock and asked if I'd seen his father. He said he'd been expecting him to call in.' Sarah Twilling twiddled the hem of her tweed skirt.

'He still could have seen your husband earlier?'

'Well, yes. He could've. Do you know all I cared about last night was that the dinner was ruined?' said Sarah Twilling. She let out a sob.

'Have you got someone you can phone to be with you?' asked the policewoman.

'Yes, I've a sister. She'll come across.'

'Thank you, Mrs Twilling,' said Campbell.

'I can't identify the body. Please don't ask me to do that.' Mrs Twilling started to sob as the policemen left. The policewoman steered Mrs Twilling back to the settee from which she'd strayed and sat down next to her.

'A small framed woman,' commented Campbell once inside the car.

'But Sarah Twilling wanted his money and now she's got it,' added Parnold.

Campbell looked at Parnold and listened to the thoughts inside his head. 'Could we call at the gatehouse?' he asked while wondering if this young man was going to worry at every thread of a clue, like a puppy with a rag. And, like a puppy, was he just going to pull the rag to pieces and run off with his favourite strand?

'Yes, Sir. The gate house it is.'

Despite the early hour Jonathan Twilling stood in jeans, jumper and green wellingtons at his gate. The delicate frosty grass damaged by his feet made a pattern to his arched front door. His fair skin had turned acutely pink in the sharp air. His short, pale yellow hair was spiked where he'd run his fingers through it.

He nodded to the policemen getting out of their car. 'I heard your car go up an hour ago. What's the matter? No one calls this early. It's about my father, isn't it?'

'Are you Mr Jonathan Twilling?' asked Parnold.

'I am.'

'I'm afraid we've found a body which has been initially identified as that of your father.' Parnold's voice was flat and emotionless. He could have been reading the news.

'The old sod.' Jonathan Twilling rubbed his chin. 'How did he go? Heart attack? No, that would have been too kind for him.'

'I'm afraid he was murdered, Mr Twilling.'

'Hah,' said Jonathan Twilling. 'He had it coming.'

'You don't seem upset about your father's death, Mr Twilling?' Campbell wondered.

'I hated him. He was a greedy cruel man. He manipulated people,' said Jonathan Twilling. 'He sent my mother insane and nearly did the same to me. He's kept Sarah up there without company for the two months they've been there. He would complain if she left the house except on his bidding, so she just stayed there.'

'You could've visited her?' suggested Campbell.

'No way. She married him for his money. She can stew in it for all I care,' replied Jonathan Twilling.

'So you aren't involved in your father's business?' asked Campbell.

'Yes, of course I am. I had to be. Everyone had to do what he wanted. He made sure of that.'

'You could have left?' Campbell's head moved down but his gaze remained in contact with Jonathan Twilling's own.

'So he could leave all his money to that thieving bitch.' Jonathan nodded towards the mansion. 'No way.'

'Has your father left his business to you?'

'That was what he said he would do. The house will be hers and some cash.'

'Mr Twilling, what were your movements last evening?' asked Campbell.

'I had a friend round for drinks, Kelvin Silverton. He's a solicitor. He handles my father's business. He came at eight o'clock. He stayed a bit longer than he'd intended. It was nearly midnight before he left.'

'Mrs Twilling said you phoned her about nine o'clock?'

'Yes I did. I'd seen my father going out for a walk.' Jonathan Twilling looked towards the entrance to the drive as he spoke. Fine gravel spread across from it onto the road, which had brought Campbell and Parnold to the Twilling homes. 'He passed here a bit before half-past six. I said to him to call in on his way back, and I told him Kelvin would be here, but he didn't turn up. It's dark by seven fifteen now. It seemed odd he should still be out walking. Of course, I thought, he could be trying to avoid me. That's why I phoned Sarah.'

'Why might he be avoiding you?' queried Campbell.

'Because he's like that, that's all.'

'Which way did your father go for his walk last evening?' asked Campbell.

Jonathan Twilling stepped out of his gate and walked out to the narrow road. He pointed northwards along it. Both Campbell and Parnold registered that the indicated direction would have taken him towards the main Hillvill, Ouse Crossing road not far from where Mrs Fenman's car had stopped, not far from the scene of his death.

'How was he walking?' asked Campbell.

'He was just walking.'

'Slow or fast,' explained Parnold.

'Fast for him, but he wasn't an athlete.'

Jonathan Twilling suddenly looked wan as if fatigue or shock had overcome him. Campbell saw him waver. 'It's cold out here, Mr Twilling. Go inside and have a warm drink. Get a friend or relative round for company.'

Jonathan Twilling had reached the door and had his hand on the latch when Parnold asked, 'Did your father have many enemies?'

'Did he have any friends? I mean real friends, not just those he'd bought?' With that, Jonathan Twilling entered the gate house and slammed the door.


A lone figure came through the double doors which seemed to fight the slender man. The hospital doors might have won but for Campbell who held one open and waited for Mr Fenman to seat himself shabbily on the low, foam padded, plastic-covered seat. Fenman might have been tall except for his stooped stance. Campbell took the seat beside him, hunched himself over and leaned his elbows on his knees. In this way his face was level with Robert Fenman's. He looked into the younger man's tired brown eyes set in the face of a man of under forty years but with an already steel grey wedge of hair falling over his eyes.

'Mr Fenman, could you tell me the events leading up to your discovery of the body?' It was pleasant to rely on training, routine and general experience. He reminded himself to pay attention to the answers, because underneath the layers of exterior calm and apparent near boredom the adrenalin was starting to pump. And that could stop him from listening carefully. Every clue was needed to prevent another life being taken.

'I didn't find it. My wife did.'

'Ah,' said Campbell glancing up. WPC Garden was standing with her bottom as close to the radiator as she could without losing her police-womanly stance. 'Go on.' added Campbell.

'She, my wife, was late home. She'd been visiting her mother.'

'What's her mother's name and where does she live?' asked Campbell surprising himself at the direct question.

'Evelyn Bane. Doctor Evelyn Bane. She's a doctor at the Hillvill surgery. She lives in Tonne Road. Is this necessary?'

'Yes, sir.' Campbell wrote these details in his notebook. He found the hospital corridor cold despite the air being hot.

'My wife was late. I was worried about her.'

'Why?'

'She says her mother's not well. She worries about her. I don't know why, she's as strong as an ox and she's got George.'

'Why didn't you phone?'

'I did, but there was no reply.'

'Who's George?'

'George Robinson. He lives there.'

'Where?'

'With Catherine's mother.' The man sounded exasperated. As if responding to his tone Campbell changed his track of questioning.

'How did you get to, shall we call it, the scene of the crime?'

'On my bike. I have a bicycle. We share a car, Inspector. My wife's teaches part time at the local school. I'm only a Development Officer at the Council. I have two young girls and we have a semi-detached town house. Now you know all there is to know about Mr Average Fenman. My wife is in there in shock. Please?'

The man was straining to go back into the ward where his wife was being nursed. Campbell let him go. He nodded to WPC Garden who dutifully followed Mr Fenman into the ward. Later would do. He started to walk away.

'Inspector,' a cheerful Asian male doctor moved neatly through the barrier of the swing doors. 'Mrs Fenman is in shock, but you will be able to talk to her in a couple of hours.'

'Yes, thank you, Doctor. WPC Garden informed me of Mrs Fenman's condition,' replied Campbell

The doctor shook Campbell's hand over firmly. 'Mrs Fenman's reaction is very severe under the circumstances. I think it is more than a simple shock at finding a dead body.'

'It must have been a gruesome experience,' said Campbell.

'I have had some experience of allergies,' said the doctor.

'Allergies?'

'Her reaction could be due to contact with an allergen,' explained the doctor. 'As soon as she can talk I'm sure she will tell us what affects her. Her husband knows she suffers from allergies, but, I'm afraid, he cannot tell us which chemicals cause problems for her.'

'Will she be O.K.?' asked Campbell looking into the doctor's eyes. Dark, honest, hardworking eyes looked back. But Campbell's nut brown irises narrowed his pupils to pierce deeper until the doctor shuffled his feet and moved his head.

'Yes, she is improving all the time even without treatment. Come back in a couple of hours, Inspector.'

'Do these things run in families? No-one in my family suffers from anything like that,' said Campbell.

'Not necessarily, Inspector,' said the Doctor sliding back through the double doors as nimbly as he'd come out of them.

The corridor was suddenly empty. Pictures of different people's lives were rattling around in Campbell's. He paced evenly down the corridor and out to the car park. In his mind he squinted at them but they were like shadows in the smoke, opaque and not fully formed.

Without searching he spotted Parnold's car parked in the far right hand side of the car park. The crisp morning had turned into a bright day as summer tried to hang onto its glory for just a little longer.

Parnold was opening his lunch box so Campbell leaned across and took one of his colleague's sandwiches.

'Parnold,' said Campbell surprising himself at remembering the young man's name. He had always addressed subordinates as 'You' in the past to save himself from a lot of confusion. 'Go and get Fenman's cycle. I want you to ride it between his house and the place where Mrs Fenman stopped, and time it. Before you do that, check out Jonathan Twilling's alibi.' He reached into the open box and took another sandwich and ate it thoughtfully. 'You can drop me off by Jonathan Twilling's cottage. I'm going for a walk.'

At the gate house Campbell took his own lunch box from the car, checked that Parnold had Kelvin Silverton's address, glanced at his over-sized watch and said again, 'Don't forget to time yourself.' Parnold's face twisted itself between a polite smile and a 'You've told me that already' expression. The result was a tight grimace. Campbell saw it and said 'Good day,' to Parnold and set off in the same direction Frederick Twilling had been seen to take.

# Chapter 3

Catherine was there. Sleep had dislocated time. Her dream was reality. For her it was lunch time, the day before the night she'd found the body. The place was the Town Hall car park. She knew this place. She knew her husband would linger here. It wasn't scenic, but her husband would try to put off the moment when he would have to meet the public. He would use any excuse to hover around the cars, from lost files to lost keys. He was not alone in this activity, some other council workers would also behave in this way. This parking area was unlike the shoppers' car park opposite, where people moved on hastily after ramming the car next to them. What a blessing her husband would find these steamed up windows: it would take him at least another ten minutes to demist them. It took her only a moment.

While she was doing this she caught a glimpse of herself in the rear view mirror and saw her own pale grey eyes – not blue in this light. They looked older than thirty two. She tried to console herself that at least her body was firm from exercise even if she did carry some weight over her broad bone structure.

She turned away from the mirror and wound down her side window to talk to her husband.

'Evelyn depends on me,' she said to him. It was an excuse. She felt obliged to her mother and the obligation was strong, though she didn't know why. And she felt it would be a sign of weakness to admit it. She had no intention of appearing weak in front of her husband. However, the argument seemed to have ended before it'd began. Robert was already standing back in the doorway of the Town Hall. He wasn't even looking at her. He was watching three men across the street. Catherine slammed the car door. Robert looked towards her slowly.

'Don't forget to get the children from Sadie's. She's collecting them from school.'

He did not answer. He was still watching the three men. Catherine followed his look. One was Robert's boss, Executive Planner for Ouseland Council, one was Frederick Twilling, property owner and developer. And, the third man, who was slightly taller than the other two, she didn't know. She squinted at him. He was wearing brown tweed instead of grey. Was it her dream or was it reality that he didn't look quite so smug as the others, though he occupied his space completely? His self-importance seemed more insular. He felt himself superior to the other two. Was it that he did not measure himself by the cut of his shabbier suit or his worn soft brown shoes? Perhaps, perhaps not. She could only see a quarter of this man's face, but this stranger's head had a raised brown mole the size of a coin on its bald crown.

The torture on her husband's face scratched at her emotions. She suddenly felt guilty and angry: all this misery for three grey men. And how grossly out of proportion their feelings of importance were with reality, she thought. How their petty officialdom had bloated their egos and their stomachs. It straightened their backs and caused smug expressions to smooth their flabby jowls.

Catherine looked back at her husband.

His back was bowed under the weight of his miseries. Was it the conflicts of his work that made him this way or was she to blame? She remembered the proud strong man she'd married. At some point, or gradually, he had retreated inside himself folding his self-pity around him, excluding Catherine, his children and the rest of the world.

'I've got to go,' she said and turned the ignition key. The car reluctantly gasped into life and carried her away from the scene. It choked slightly at the junction. She used it as an excuse to put her foot flat on the accelerator and make the engine roar. She took the Hillvill turn and tried to neutralise her brain by concentrating on the tarmac.

Beyond the town the forest began immediately on both sides of the road. Her dream distorted the darkness of the shady interior cast by the trees. So relief spread through her as her dream brought her to where the far side of the road opened into open fields lined with black poplars. Their yellow leaves made a golden band in the afternoon sunshine.

But her thoughts niggled back into her dreaming consciousness. He was jealous, she was sure of it. She knew she was right, so why did she feel cruel to think such thoughts? His own mother was dead so he didn't want her to have Evelyn. That was clear. Though, she didn't really have Evelyn as a mother.

A hamlet appeared after the forest. Then open fields spread out until Hillvill started abruptly with a new housing estate, a bypass and a business park of glass and steel which had business emblems flapping with the authority of national flags along the front. The Twilling building stood proud in the front of the complex – one of only half the buildings which were occupied.

Catherine turned right at the traffic lights onto Tonne Road. This road ran along a hillside overlooking the fens. From the first floor windows of the houses on this road an expanse of flat fields could be seen spreading far into the distance, with the ever changing sky dictating the mood of the landscape. Every detail of the place was in sharp focus. It was as if her mind was searching for the well-known places of her childhood to try to comfort her in her sleep.

Most of the town avoided the river at the bottom of the hill. Only a few poor cottages dared to be so close to the ancient risk of flood. Even modern buildings were missing from this area despite the flood risk having been reduced in the last thirty years by the building of cuts and dykes, drains and sluices. In the town itself, which Catherine avoided if she could, the yellow bricked buildings were greyed by grime and had black slate roofs made uneven by their poor repair. The buildings were mostly two storey with the odd three storey building in between. A hundred years ago these would have been important busy places, now many of them were empty with bare and broken upper windows. On the ground floor the buildings were shops fitted with modern windows displaying modern goods denying the decay above them. The wealthy business people now inhabited red brick and red tiled houses on the outskirts of the town. Though Tonne Road was not such an outskirt, it had been left unchanged since before the Second World War. Catherine shook her head. She did not even like to think about the town she was brought up in. There was no comfort there.

Further on, with mixed feelings, she turned into her mother's yard.

Evelyn was pretending to do some gardening, but both of them knew she was waiting for her daughter. The tall woman straightened as she heard the car roll onto the tarmac yard. Her short curly hair – dressed in a style which was a careful compromise between fashions twenty years ago and modernity – bobbed above the roses. It suited her well, and her smile would have seemed genuine to anyone but her daughter. Catherine replied with something similar and they hugged. The contact was only physical. As the distance between them grew again, Catherine relaxed slightly.

'Where's George, Evelyn?' She'd found it impossible to call this woman 'Mother' to her face, or any term on those lines. They both found the use of her first name acceptable.

'In the greenhouse,' was the brusque reply.

'And Kimber?' asked Catherine looking around for the dog.

'He's dead,' Evelyn replied walking into the kitchen to make a cup of tea.

What was that about death? She remembered something about death, but what was it? The smell of smoke in her lungs or was it something else, giddiness and a forest...

Catherine awoke sweating and chilled. The hospital invaded her senses. Robert leaned over her. He didn't have to say anything. The love in his eyes touched her somewhere inside and calmed her, but it couldn't take away the feeling that death was close.

'They're going to think we did it, Robert,' she whispered in her husband's ear. There was no logic to her words, she knew that, but hadn't someone once said that the person who finds the body can be suspected of the crime? 'They're going to think we murdered that man.'

Robert made comforting noises, but she could feel he too was fighting a sense of guilt. She pulled him close and drew his scent into her body. It could still give her strength, and it filled a lonely, empty space inside her. She wasn't sure if it was love she felt, but she knew it was need. To stop holding him at that moment would be to let go of part of her life.

# Chapter 4

Campbell felt refreshed mentally, but the effects of the sandwich box were wearing off. He'd reached the scene of Frederick Twilling's death and had found a police car to take him back to the office. He had already ensconced himself in a room, which was not his own office. It contained someone else's soup. He was eating it when Parnold came in. The younger man's once impeccable suit looked crumpled and grubby. There was a greasy streak in the pattern of a bicycle chain across the bottom of his right trouser from the exercise Campbell had bidden him carry out. He realised he should ask Parnold how it went, but he didn't.

'Inspector Campbell?'

'Yes.' Campbell wondered if his stomach would ever get used to eating supper at lunch time. He put the soup down.

'Here's the list of local slaughter men you asked for and there's a Mr Donald Mercer outside wishing to speak with you. He's from Ouseland District Council. He knew Mr Frederick Twilling.'

'Thank you. Send him through.' Campbell picked up the list of slaughter men. They were all past and present employees of the local abattoir.

'And send a team to question all these people.' He looked at the young man as if he would trust him with his soul. Parnold took the list with something close to gratitude.

Uninvited, Donald Mercer took himself straight from the door to a seat opposite Campbell. Campbell was energetically rubbing his right hand with his left.

'I've got cramp. It comes and goes,' Campbell explained while he absorbed the characteristics of the man before him. Was he just another grey official? That's what he looked like. He raised his head, neat as a hazel nut, to meet his visitor's pasty blue eyes. 'You knew Mr Twilling?'

'Yes. But I've come about Fenman,' said Mercer. Campbell noted that the muscles around the man's mouth tweaked on the 'T' sound, making his jowls wrinkle.

'Fenman?'

'Robert Fenman. I'm his manager. There was an incident between him and Mr Twilling on the day Mr Twilling died.' Mercer emphasised the 'ee' sounds too, Campbell noted, so he pronounced 'between' as 'betweeen'. He wondered if Mercer did it to give authority to his words. He found it irritating.

'Yes?' queried Campbell.

'Mr Twilling claimed Robert Fenman'd hit him that morning during a meeting they'd had at the site of a proposed housing development on the edge of Ouse Crossing.'

'Oh?' said Campbell sounding particularly Scottish and rubbing his hand again.

'Are you listening, man?' Mercer growled. 'This isn't easy.'

'Ay,' said Campbell, continuing to rub his hand. 'So?'

'So, that afternoon, I suspended Fenman pending the private prosecution Mr Twilling was going to bring against him,' said Mercer.

'Against Fenman?' Campbell sought clarification.

'Yes,' confirmed Mercer.

'I see,' said Campbell. 'Why didn't Frederick Twilling come to the police?'

'I don't know why,' Mercer replied.

'He wouldn't get far if he hadn't pursued that possibility, Mr Mercer. Perhaps Frederick Twilling's threats were empty?'

'Mr Twilling was a very important man. He wouldn't make empty accusations.'

'Wouldn't he?' persisted Campbell.

'No.' Mercer sighed and relaxed back in his chair, so Campbell asked,

'What was your relationship like with Frederick Twilling?'

'Only professional. He was a developer. And Mrs Twilling is a councillor, but you knew that, of course?' There no reply so he continued. 'She was a councillor before she married Mr Twilling, while she was still Mrs Petry.'

'That's a great chair,' said Campbell rising to indicate the interview was over. 'I can't get anyone to sit in it though. I found it dumped at the tip. By the way, where were you last night?'

'At home,' said Mercer rapidly leaving the chair and viewing it with distaste. 'It must be a terrible responsibility to have to catch a murderer.' Mercer narrowed his eyes. 'If you get it wrong you leave a killer loose in the community.'

'I have every intention of catching the perpetrator of this crime, Sir,' said Campbell. He wanted to say 'as soon as possible', but he realised that might sound as if he could do the job quickly. This man was annoying him so he moved over to the door and called, 'Someone?'

WPC Jenner appeared. 'Take a statement from Mr Mercer,' and as Mercer passed into the outer office he added, 'And check it out.'

'I've been informed of your relationship with Mr Frederick Twilling,' said Campbell to Catherine Fenman's husband. The level of light inside the hospital corridor was unchanged from earlier in the day despite the shifting of the sun. Robert Fenman put his newspaper down on the seat between himself and Campbell. Mr Twilling's picture had made the afternoon edition. 'They're quick getting these stories in the paper,' Campbell remarked. 'Been on the TV too, I expect.'

'I bet Mercer's been round to see you,' said Robert Fenman referring to Campbell's first remark. 'He couldn't wait to tell you about Frederick Twilling and me. It's all lies. I didn't hit him yesterday morning. He didn't like it because I'm not in his pocket or in awe of him. I told him his proposed development went against all the guidelines.'

'How do you mean?' asked Campbell, pleased to find his subject in a talkative mood.

'The site is beautiful. It has wonderful views. It is a bit of a distance out of town and we have enough sites put aside already in Ouse Crossing for industry. That man had no morals.'

'And you have?' asked Campbell.

'I didn't kill him for a lack of morals either, if that's what you mean? He had lots of enemies. You don't kill people just because they are money grabbers, Inspector. But Frederick Twilling trod on a lot of people to get into that big house.' Fenman didn't wait for Campbell to end the interview; instead he took himself back through the double doors to his wife's bedside, so Campbell loped off in search of a cup of tea and Parnold.

Having found both he returned to the hospital corridor with Parnold. It was quiet except for a nurse who told them that she thought Mr Fenman would be heading towards the canteen as she'd sent him for something to eat. It was surprising, she said, that they hadn't bumped into each other.

'Good,' said Parnold as he pushed the door open to Mrs Catherine Fenman's ward. The ward nurse stood at the nurse's station and nodded them in the direction of a curtained area among a group of six beds. The other five beds were empty.

Catherine had been dreaming again. This time she saw a small girl screaming in a car. She recognised the child as herself. Yet she was not inside the child she was watching. The child begged to know what she'd done wrong and why she was being sent away. No solace was offered by the woman driving the car, just the threat of a sedative to keep the child quiet. The driver was young, a woman in her early-twenties with long legs a heart shaped face and long wavy dark hair.

I wanted to be like her, thought the watching Catherine. I wanted her power and beauty. She wanted to comfort the not yet eight year old Catherine now sobbing in the back seat.

The picture changed. The same child was writing at a desk. She was writing a letter to her mother. It was a cheerful fantasy about her boarding school. She thought it was what her mother would want. She knew the day was not a Sunday, but it did not matter to her as every day was the same with nuns, corridors, stiff laundry and stiff faces. Her knees had developed hard pads from praying to see her mother. But Evelyn never came.

Catherine awoke and pushed her dream away. It was unpleasant and it was in the past, but then the present was a new horror. She fixed her thoughts on Robert. Once she had realised he was there that night among the blood and bracken to help her she had felt him protecting her from the fear. She could visualise his face now smiling and gentle, the way he'd looked on the birth of their first baby, Laura. It caught her up in a moment of simple love. She loved Robert then. But her imagination changed her husband's expression to one she didn't know, one of murderous cruelty. The smell of smoke returned, filling her nostrils and catching in her throat. She opened her eyes, squinted at the policemen and tried to sit up.

Inside the pastel shaded curtains WPC Garden rose slightly from her seat near Catherine Fenman. Campbell waved her and Mrs Fenman down before they were fully upright.

'Could you open the curtains, please? I could do with more air,' said

Catherine Fenman.

Campbell watched Parnold unashamedly scrutinize the woman in bed. He looked at her too. He concentrated on her face and saw the rest of her without moving his eyes. Her bone structure was angular but well padded. Her square jaw line was warm but efficient. But her face looked lost in hospital. It was a face where open friendliness would have been at home under different circumstances, Campbell decided. But she was strongly built despite her allergies, a sports woman, perhaps? Campbell tried to engage her by gently focusing on her. A smile wasn't appropriate but his face softened. Catherine Fenman's gaze wandered about the room clearly trying to take in the people about her.

The events came out of her in a jumble of words. The words seem unattached to any reality. A gentle drift of noise. The real words seemed to be stuck inside. Campbell wondered how he could get at them.

'You didn't recognise your husband when you saw him in the forest, Mrs Fenman?' he asked gently.

'I don't know why. I suppose it was because I felt woozy. It was dark,' she replied.

'Had you been drinking?' asked Parnold. She shook her head.

'The blood sample was clear,' cut in Campbell. Parnold knew that. He frowned at him. 'Your clothes have been taken away for forensic tests,' Campbell explained to the patient.

'I know,' said Catherine. 'Someone came in to collect them. I've got another set of clothes from home. My husband got them for me. He had to get some things for himself as they took his too. "To eliminate any fibres from our clothes they might find at the scene of the crime," the woman said.'

'Yes, that's it,' agreed Campbell. 'Your children, where were they while all this was going on?'

'My girls were staying with my friend Sadie Groom and they are with her now.' Mrs Fenman almost smiled as she talked of her offspring.

'What shoes were you wearing?' asked Parnold.

'Trainers,' she replied.

'What size?' asked Parnold.

'Seven, but your forensic people took those too.'

'Thank you,' said Campbell.

'How did you run out of petrol?' asked Parnold. There was a pinking of the ears and a slight flush on the sergeant's neck.

'I hadn't taken much note of the petrol gauge as the tank was full when I picked it up from my husband at the council offices that lunch time.'

'Have you had a cold?' Parnold asked this question too. Campbell tutted at his colleague's underlying aggression. He guessed that Catherine Fenman's physical and mental strength would be incapable of strain. Truth could come from an exhausted mind, but the body could collapse taking the mind with it.

'No,' she said quietly.

'There was a strong smell of eucalyptus in the car,' said Parnold. Campbell had allowed him to continue, though Parnold had not noticed whether he'd been given consent or not.

'I don't use anything like that. I'm allergic to the smell. It makes me feel terrible. Oh, so it wasn't smoke,' she said, a note of realisation and sorrow in her voice. Campbell looked away from her face. 'I remember a smell before I became woozy,' she added. 'In my dreams it seems to be smoke, but there wasn't any smoke. You're right. There was a smell of eucalyptus. It overcame me.'

'Who would do that to you?' asked Parnold.

'You mean it could have been put there on purpose?' asked Catherine Fenman.

Campbell nodded.

'My husband had the car in the morning and he usually makes several visits during that time. In the afternoon I was at my mother's. It was parked outside and it was unlocked then too. But perhaps someone just dropped something in there by accident.'

'What do you mean by "too", Mrs Fenman,' asked Parnold.

'The car's often unlocked. When my husband's on a visit he doesn't always lock it,' said Catherine Fenman. She looked tired.

'Isn't it unlikely that someone dropped some eucalyptus by accident?' Parnold's voice was getting louder.

'My husband often takes other people in his car.' Catherine Fenman's jaw moved forward. She looked defiantly at Parnold. 'Work colleagues, students.'

'Could your husband have left something like that in the car?' persisted Parnold.

'He hasn't got a cold.' A mist of sweat appeared on the invalid's forehead.

'Couldn't your husband have murdered Mr Frederick Twilling, Mrs

Fenman? Mrs Fenman, he could have wanted you out of the way too so he could be with your friend, Sadie Groom. But you ran out of petrol before you had an accident. He could have set up an alibi with Sadie? Then you found the body and upset his plans?' Parnold weaselled, 'Don't you think that is what could have happened? Your husband and Sadie Groom?'

Campbell watched Catherine Fenman's mouth shut and her face close against her inquisitor. A moment later she was gasping for breath and the policemen were being pushed away by medical staff.

As Campbell and Parnold passed back through the ward doors, Robert Fenman appeared at the far end of the corridor, his long strides covering the distance between them and him. He looked at their faces. Campbell saw him read some difficulty with his wife on them.

'What's happened?' Fenman asked, and then he swore. 'What have you done to her?' He didn't wait for a reply, but pushed through the doors towards his wife.

'That was a bit unnecessary,' said Campbell to Parnold meaning his questioning of Catherine Fenman.

'I'm sorry,' replied the younger man. It seemed he knew without being told what Campbell meant. 'I get so impatient with your round the houses type questioning.'

'It's those questions that get answers. Your questions place your theories onto a set of very incomplete circumstances. It's like trying to make a landscape jigsaw out of the pieces from a seascape.' Campbell looked at Parnold and he knew he hadn't heard. 'You have to have the right pieces and they have to fit to get the right picture.' Campbell found he was speaking mostly to himself.

Parnold's words were rattling at him. Campbell closed his eyes. It didn't stop him from listening. The sound of the car rumbled beneath him giving womb-like comfort.

'It's got to be Robert Fenman,' said Parnold. 'I've spoken with Sadie Groom. He was meant to pick his children up after work from her. He never did. He was alone that night. He got to the forest first, met Frederick Twilling, murdered him and was just going home when his wife ran out of petrol at that very spot. In a horrible coincidence his wife found the body.'

'Mr Fenman is a man of morals. He said so,' said Campbell without commitment in his voice.

'Perhaps he thought he was ridding the world of an evil man. His conscience would be clear if he thought it justified,' said Parnold.

'Drop me off here, Parnold,' said Campbell. He was ready to have a rest from twisting and turning his thoughts into lines and stars, relating and linking the facts he had. There were too few pieces of the puzzle to make any recognisable shape. 'I'll walk the rest of the way home.' They'd come to a rough lane that forked off a sharp bend in the road. The pinks and purples in the sky were powerful against the thinning autumn trees. The oak trees, however, still hung onto their leaves, Campbell noticed. He knew he would enjoy the walk down the lane to his cottage. He stepped out knowing the case was behind him with Parnold, while in front of him were a warm home and his wife, Margaret.

Campbell toyed with the idea of putting up another half dozen tiles in the bathroom before bed. His working day from eight thirty last night until four this afternoon had left him tired, but wound up. He knew each tile would gently untie his knotted nerves and he would sleep better for it.

Margaret was looking at brochures of Scotland when he walked in the door. He gave her the look he always gave her when she wanted to go visit her family north of the border. He would not go. He'd never taken the time to look back. He didn't want to. All he wanted was to solve crimes. It meant there was no time to think about the past. She and the children could go, but he would not. She understood. She always understood and not a word had been said.

A leaflet about Campbell's Castle fluttered out of the pile. Margaret picked it up. The powerful stone semi-ruined castle beckoned enticingly above the leafy glen. Raymond Campbell turned away from this idyll. For his Scotland was not full of happy holiday memories of childhood and never would be.

After an early tea Margaret started grouting the tiles around the shower while he tiled over the basin.

After Campbell had put up three tiles Margaret said, 'There's something wrong with the car. It's not running right.'

'Can you manage with it for now?' he asked.

'I suppose so,' she said.

'I'll look at it tomorrow.' Campbell completed one more tile, wandered into the living room and fell asleep on the settee, despite his complaining teenagers trying to play their music at him. 'Do your homework,' he muttered drowsily before he slept.

❋         ❋         ❋

Campbell's dream was a sorting dream. He was waiting in a bus queue in a bus shelter sandwiched between Sarah Twilling and Jonathan Twilling, wife and son of Frederick, who were whispering to each other behind his back. Mrs Twilling was wearing her brown suit and Jonathan cord trousers wax-cotton coat and green wellingtons. Beyond them, the Fenmans were staggering about in the street, the pouring rain soaking their blood stained clothes. Campbell saw this picture, including himself in the queue, from afar and told himself it had not rained last night, so what was it doing raining in his dream. The Campbell in the queue pushed past Sarah Twilling in front of him and looked at the time table fixed to the bus shelter. It was ripped. The half that remained said:

18-30 Frederick Twilling walks

19-00 Catherine Fenman leaves her mother's

19-15 Dark

19-30 Runs out of petrol

19-45 Catherine Fenman gets out of car

20-30 Police called

21-00 Jonathan phones Sarah Twilling

Other people were moving towards the queue. Some were dressed in white and some were carrying knives. Campbell could not make out their faces. They seemed only interested in pushing and shoving each other. They didn't even notice Campbell in the queue.

Which one was the murderer, wondered the watching Campbell. Would he know in time to prevent another death? Somehow his dreaming self knew there would be another murder.

He started to walk from the queue through the fiery gold of autumnal bracken on the hills around Campbell's Castle; the burnished trees reddening the glen. The journey to that place was through a wild tangled twisted path, the unworldliness enticing him on across uneven, slippery ground. He felt he was being diverted from the castle to be tripped up; to never get there.

# Chapter 5

At Sadie Groom's house Catherine's six year old was flopped on the floor watching television, while her eight year old was sitting on a dining room chair in front of a coffee table. Catherine smiled at their long dark blond hair made golden by the past summer, so their locks were just a shade lighter than her own jaw length hair. They did not see her until she spoke. 'I'm here,' she said opening her arms. They were immediately filled by the living bodies of her two daughters.

The six-year-old, Molly, gave herself up completely to her mother's affections. The older one, Laura, embraced with less vigour. There was confusion in Laura's movements. Catherine looked down at her. She was too young for all of this and yet too old to be protected by the direct thinking that keeps the very young almost immune to disasters. As Catherine thought this, she felt Laura's resistance to her embrace weaken. Catherine sunk herself into them, soaking up the completeness they gave her. All the misery of the last twenty four hours seeped away. Where they touched each other, their combined body heat seemed to melt the surfaces of their skins.

Catherine lifted her head over her children's shoulders and looked at Sadie. Why had the police accused Sadie? They couldn't be right. Her auburn haired friend of fifteen years knew everything about Catherine there was to know. Catherine had always told her everything and was happy to do so. She watched Sadie bend over to pick up the debris of the day. She knew her friend's own two small children were in bed. She admired Sadie. She seemed so strong among all this bedlam, continuing her motherly duties without wavering. She seemed complete despite or, perhaps, because her husband worked abroad for three months at a stretch.

She wanted to apologise for dragging Sadie into all of this but, somehow, it didn't seem necessary. They passed each other a look which explained everything while making a comment on the autumnal weather. But as Catherine picked up their jackets to go Sadie caught her arm.

'Look, you can stay here tonight, if you want. You don't have to go home,' she said.

'Yes I do. Robert's there,' said Catherine. 'I woke up at the hospital and they told me he'd gone home but would be back shortly. I got up and discharged myself. The police have got my mobile so I phoned home from a public phone box outside the hospital. I didn't get a reply, so I came straight here.'

'Get your mother over.' Catherine noted the implication in her friend's voice: what good is Robert? She didn't like it, but she was used to it. How could the police think that Sadie and Robert could be linked in the murder of Frederick Twilling? Her friend had never liked her husband, nor could that have been a pretence? Impatience flared up in her voice. 'I'll be all right, Sadie. We're only in the next street we'll give you a ring if we need to.'

Sadie nodded, but frowned. 'You must let me help. I want to.'

'I know, Sadie. You've been wonderful already.' She looked at her elegant friend. She was some inches taller than herself and her long limbs moved with a gentle grace that made Catherine feel clumsy. Just for a moment she imagined her husband entwined in those slim arms. Then she dismissed the thought.

'Good night, Sadie.'

'Good night, Cath.'

The door closed and Catherine, Molly and Laura set off for the next street. Molly zigzagged despite holding on to her mother's hand while Laura measured out each step evenly, close to the edge of the pavement. They reached the top of the street and started to pass the small corner shop, which Catherine had rarely been past late enough to see shut, when they heard a car approaching along the top road.

The car's headlights blazed an arc across the far side of the road. The children turned their heads without embarrassment to see where such a late caller would be going. Catherine also watched, more as a mother waiting for her children than as an observer. But when it stopped outside her friend's house and its tall occupant strode out and knocked on Sadie's door, she quickly lowered her eyes and drew the two girls away. The slim figure had been easy to recognise. 'Kelvin Silverton. Blast you,' she muttered.

She watched her feet attack the pavement, each step thumping out her feelings forcing Molly and Laura to run. At first she felt a tangle of unwanted despair and arid hatred for Kelvin Silverton. She remembered his cool blue eyes, short cropped dark hair and his control over his body and mind. There was no emotion in his life. Then she felt regret at her stupid naivety. All those months ago she hadn't noticed herself being charmed by the solicitor. She hadn't noticed that for him there had been no genuine interest, for him it had just been a game. And how much she had been guilty of playing a game, she didn't know. At first the affair had been an emotional escape for her, but at some stage it had changed: she too had become a decision making player in his game. All naivety had been left behind.

'I thought you said Dad was home,' said Laura pulling at Catherine's sleeve.

The stout house with its two bay windows, one above the other, was in darkness. The front door was to the right of the living room window. Next to the late Victorian semi, and set back, was a more recently built garage. Its up and over door was firmly closed. The car was still with the police, she reminded herself.

'Perhaps, he's gone to bed,' Catherine suggested while her mind gave her other possibilities, such as: he'd run away or had an accident. He'd been home earlier for their clothes, she knew that. Inside today's post and newspapers tripped her up. 'He must have come in the back way,' she said to herself.

'What did you say?' asked Laura from behind her.

'Nothing, Laura. We probably missed him. I should think he's gone back to the hospital. He'll be home later.'

With practiced automation Catherine put Molly and Laura to bed. When she tried to leave them they tugged at her and asked for cuddles. She gave what she could but still she was distracted by Kelvin Silverton's visit to her friend Sadie and the absence of Robert. She left them to arrange for her own sleep trying to believe the words she'd told her children, but the hospital was not far and he would have been here by now.

The bedroom door opened. A shaft of light from the hallway cut through the room. Two warm night-dressed bodies clambered in next to her. She closed her eyes. The children's youthful strength and beauty pushed back her waking nightmare. Perhaps, she thought, that was what George had meant.

Beauty. She smiled in her sleep. George had been right. It could be a buffer against the cruelty of the world. She hugged her children tightly and slept.

Eventually her daytime nightmares came into her sleep and despite the comfort of her children she awoke sweating. She looked around at the familiar pictures and furniture concentrating on their solidity, pushing the visions of Frederick Twilling's body away. The sunlight clipped onto her forty year old furniture, most of it bought second hand at auctions before the birth of her children. The rest had been left to them by Robert's family. None of it was valuable but the soft curves and mellow colours were warm and friendly in the morning light. She tiptoed from her room leaving Molly and Laura to sleep their fill.

In the bathroom it was cold, but the heating had just come on so the radiator was hot. She had come in here to examine herself. She would do this without a mirror. It would not be a medical examination nor a sensual one, but a check on reality. She slipped off the long t-shirt she used as a night dress and touched herself. She was surprised to find her body relaxed, comfortable and acceptable.

She washed, put on underwear and a simple jersey dress. It was unusual for her to bother with underwear but she felt vulnerable and she needed their modesty and security. Finally she pushed on her old slippers.

'Please God; bring Robert back today, she thought, as she picked up her husband's clothes from the floor. She hugged them to her burying her face in his shirt. She felt part of her was missing without him and by inhaling his scent she could put a small piece of him back inside her before placing his things in the laundry basket. Then she remembered the shirt. It was the one he'd been wearing at the hospital yesterday. So he had come back and changed a second time. The clothes had been there last night but she hadn't looked at them. They had just been dirty linen on the floor.

Catherine made her way down the stairs and counted the steps. They were still all there. She picked up yesterday's untouched newspapers from the doormat and pulled today's from the letter box. Robert had come in and gone out the back way, she was sure now.

It was too early to start phoning round to see if he was at a friend's and she didn't feel inclined to phone the police either. It was none of their business if her husband decided to leave home. They would ask why had he gone, and she wouldn't be able to say. But that Scottish policeman would come and look at her with his piercing eyes and see her guilt. How could she say that Robert had probably had enough of her? Surely the episode in the hospital had confirmed to him she was useless and neurotic as well as a slut. Or could it be worse than that, like the tall blond policeman had said. Could Robert be the murderer? No, she couldn't accept that. She couldn't let him go and it was hard to do nothing.

She fingered the newspaper. She didn't want to open it. It was a compromise between a national paper and a local rag combining the big local and national stories. She knew that it would have Frederick Twilling's death displayed on its front page. It was likely too that the press would soon be knocking on her door.

The blind in the kitchen clacked as she lifted it. It always clacked, but this morning it made her jump. She looked out on her long narrow garden. It looked a haven from the outside world. It had high fencing all round with a gate made from a fencing panel at the far end. This led into an alley that ran along the bottom of all the gardens on Catherine's side of the street. She'd planted climbing and rambling plants to disguise the fence, a lot of them were roses. Her roses came in every shade, but, perhaps, she thought, the Jacob's rose with its ever changing coloured flowers was her favourite but they were long gone, leaving ruddy hips behind them.

By the gate stood the shed. This was Robert's favourite place. It was larger than most garden sheds and contained every sort of wood working tool she could imagine. She smiled and wanted to weep. The telephone ringing in the hall stopped her.

Before she lifted it she knew it would be her mother. Evelyn spoke in tones that were a carefully calculated cross between bed-side manner, maternal sympathy and personal hurt.

'I would have told you,' 'I was asleep most of the time,' 'I didn't want to worry you,' and 'I didn't have time,' seemed pointless excuses for not phoning her mother and not telling her of the disaster, but Catherine made them all the same. And, yes, she shouldn't have let her find out from the radio.

'Come over and stay with me,' ordered the doctor.

Catherine managed to say, 'No.'

'Where's that husband of yours? Is he there?' asked Evelyn, her tone felt threatening to Catherine. She wanted to defend herself, defend her husband.

'Of course he is,' Catherine lied.

'Let me speak to him.'

'No. He's not here at the moment. He's popped out.' Catherine tried to control her voice remembering her sleeping children upstairs. She tried not to think about the truth in case her voice would tell her mother that he was gone and she was worried about him. The older woman at the other end of the line grunted. Catherine heard the grunt dismiss Robert as of no importance to the human race.

'Send the girls over, then. This sort of thing isn't good for them.'

'Not yet, Evelyn,' said Catherine. She could feel her mother's will was still stronger than her own and it was eating away at her resolve. She wanted her family, what there was of it, to be together. It gave them strength. There was a silence which was questioning on her mother's part and with-holding on Catherine's.

'All right then,' said Evelyn and a loud click ended the conversation from her end of the telephone line. Catherine put down her receiver. She knew her mother was important but her problems would have to wait. At the moment she was only complicating matters.

Catherine caught herself smiling over Evelyn's cranky behaviour as she returned to the kitchen. She had just reached the sink when the gate at the bottom of the garden moved. It opened slightly and half a face appeared from behind it. The glimpse she'd got was of a pixie-featured woman with dark straggly hair poking out of a grubby scarf. Catherine swore, flung herself at the back door, rattled the key in the lock as she turned it, and rushed down her stepping-stone path to the gate. She flung the gate open.

The pixie-woman squinted up at her as if she should have worn glasses. 'Your gate was open, Mrs Fenman,' wheedled the woman.

'Go away,' said Catherine, slamming the gate shut. She shoved the wheelbarrow against it. She tried to settle herself but there was something else out of place. She couldn't see or hear anything. Perhaps it was a smell.

The shed was unlocked. She pulled open the door and looked inside.

Frederick Twilling's body hanging from the tree was now over-laid with an identical reality. But without her brain poisoned by chemicals she could see it all clearly, not swirling in imagined smoke. The first horror had partially deadened her senses to this repeat, so she managed to control her weakened limbs and keep her throat from screaming.

Robert had installed a beam in the shed with a block and tackle for lifting heavy objects. Underneath a man was hanging upside down. He was clothed in a subtle but expensive suit. His back was to her, but his face was looking at her. His shock of dark hair and his features would have been unrecognisable to most people because of the splattered blood, but Catherine knew them too well. Even in this state she could see who it was.

'Kelvin.' Her mouth made the word, but no sound came out.

The body's heart had stopped beating and the wooden shed floor was covered in tacky blood. Catherine staggered back over the door step and shut the shed, snapping the padlock shut.

Coldness came over her face and neck, spread down through her breasts and over her stomach, which pulled and pushed at its emptiness.

This thing violated her home, her garden, and her children. But why? This made her and Robert look guilty. At least it wasn't Robert hanging there with his throat cut. Only now she would have to call the police. And they would point to his absence. Could her husband have murdered these two men to punish her? Could he have arranged for the petrol to run out and the eucalyptus in the car? 'Please, God, no.'

A gentle piping voice came from the back door. The realisation of her daughters calling to her made her collect her thoughts and straighten her body. Catherine slipped off her sodden slippers and walked back along the spaced paving slabs. Each foot left a dark red print behind it. Before her girls could look more carefully at her feet she shoved them into a pair of Robert's slippers which always stood just inside the door.

'Are you all right, Mummy?' asked Laura. Both girls were looking into Catherine's face searching for truth and reassurance. Catherine knew these things were not the same and tried to provide the latter by saying, 'Yes, I'm fine.' Molly and Laura seemed to accept the lie, but only as it came from her and she knew they could tell it was a lie. Catherine rested a hand on each of their shoulders while she steered them and herself away from the back door and into the house.

She sat them down in the living room and returned to the hall leaving the door open so they could see her. She dialled the emergency number. It struck her how alien it felt. She'd never dialled it before. Robert had phoned for the police at the cottage in the forest. The thought suddenly struck her that the simple faced woman from the cottage would probably never be closer to a horror than allowing others hit by disaster to use her phone. It wasn't fair.

Holding the receiver tightly, Catherine heard the phone at the other end ring twice before it was answered. But she was not listening; her thoughts had turned back to the corpse. The woman at the other end was asking which service she wanted and her telephone number. She supplied the information in a dazed whisper and then explained to the police why she required them.

It must have only taken the police a few minutes to get there, but in that time Catherine helped the girls dress and she threw some things in a couple of suitcases.

'We're going to stay with Sadie,' she explained to Laura and Molly as she went into the bathroom. She didn't even want to think that Robert and Sadie might be entwined in this evil slaughter. Yet Robert was not here.

'Complete nonsense,' she added.

Catherine convinced herself that what she really needed was the comfort and support Sadie could give her.

She slipped off one of Robert's slippers and balanced with the bare foot in the basin while she tried to wash blood from between her toes. She was still in this position when there was a firm rap at the door.

She heard Laura answer it and tell the mêlée of policemen and women to come in. It sounded as if the girl's tense nervousness had been replaced by cool control. Catherine came down the stairs with one clean bare foot and one still bloodied and in her husband's slipper. She hoped her daughter's control was real and not just a brittle facade. She touched the girl's shoulder. Yes, she could feel the difference. This was real.

"Please, Robert," she said inside her head, "Come home."

# Chapter 6

'You've finished my tiling!' complained Campbell. His Edinburgh accent was particularly strong in the mornings. It struck him that Margaret was either pretending she couldn't hear, didn't understand, or both.

'Sergeant Parnold's here for you,' she said.

'Don't let him in.'

'I have to, Raymond.' Campbell heard his wife's voice match his own in calling on its Celtic roots for authority.

'No you don't.' Campbell returned to his bathroom to finish his ablutions and to watch Parnold, who retreated from the front door and sat in his car. He heard Margaret close the front door and he guessed Parnold would be sulking. He glanced at his watch. There had already been rattles on the door for use of the bathroom. The moment he came out the near naked body of his only-just-teenage son flashed in. He descended the stairs coming to terms with the fact he would have to leave his home and go to work.

In the dining room Margaret was lifting a mound of papers and pieces of fabric onto the dining room table.

Raymond Campbell picked a piece of flimsy paper from the floor and placed it on the table as he went through the dining room. When he reached the front door he turned back to his wife, he said, 'Don't use the car unless you have to. I'll look at it when I get back.' He closed the door without waiting for a reply and walked down the garden path without enthusiasm. The digital clock in Parnold's car said eight hundred hours.

'Inspector, I brought you an initial report from forensic on the Fenmans' car and of the crime scene. I think you ought to read it,' offered Parnold.

37

'That means you've already read it,' Campbell said. His eyelids barely twitched with irritation.

'Yes, Sir.' Parnold's voice was eager.

'Well?' asked Campbell.

'Firstly, there was a hole in the petrol tank of the Fenman's car. The driver's window was stuck and wouldn't open. It looked like wear and tear, apparently. And it seems the footprint belongs to Catherine Fenman. And, you know the blue rope which was used to hang up the victim, Sir?'

Campbell felt himself nod his head like a puppet and open his eyes at Parnold's words. The young man continued, losing his local accent as he spoke, 'Traces of the same rope were found in the Fenman's car boot.' Campbell mused that Parnold might be trying to sound like a news reader.

'It's common rope, Parnold,' said Campbell scanning the pages of the report. 'It's the sort a lot of people carry in the boot of their car for towing.'

'But look at Mrs Fenman's statement,' Parnold persisted. 'She said she went to the boot for a petrol can and there was nothing there. She said herself there was usually a tow rope, a can of petrol, a torch and a few tools lying in the boot. I bet you if we show Mrs Fenman the torch that was with the body, the one she picked up, she'll identify it as hers.' Campbell heard Parnold's enthusiasm push out his news reading voice and let in his Norfolk brogue.

'I expect you have it with you?' asked Campbell.

'Yes, Sir.'

'I think we'd better call on the Fenmans,' said Campbell.

'Yes, Sir. Exactly, Sir.' Parnold started the car and surged to the top of the lane churning light sand dust into the air. He braked hard at the top to avoid hitting a lorry. Campbell braced himself for a rough ride.

A couple of miles out from Ouse Crossing Parnold accelerated over a humped back bridge. Campbell saw before him a tractor facing them and the rear of a chocolate brown Rolls Royce. He closed his eyes and counted. Almost immediately he was pitched forward as Parnold performed an emergency stop. For a moment he thought he might die, but he opened his eyes to see a vaguely familiar woman in a black suit and low heels standing between the Rolls Royce and the tractor.

'Mrs Twilling,' yelled Parnold from the car. 'Could you move your car, please?' The radio broke in half-way through Parnold's yell. It told them that Mrs Fenman had found a body in her garden shed.

Campbell removed himself from the car. 'Good morning, Mrs Twilling,' he said as he walked around the front of the Rolls Royce. 'Good morning, Burt,' he addressed the tractor driver agreeably. He recognised the local farmer. Campbell could hear Mrs Twilling hurling whining complaints at the old boy. Campbell glanced at her. The forty-five year old's immaculate face was crumpled and tears were welling up in her eyes. As he stood in front of Mrs Twilling he could see Parnold screwing his hands around the steering wheel of his car. 'It's not so cold this morning,' remarked Campbell.

Mrs Twilling stopped whining and wiped her face with a lace handkerchief. 'I'm sorry, Inspector, I don't know what came over me,' she apologised. 'Here I am behaving like my husband. Whatever for? It wouldn't have taken a moment to pull over, but I wouldn't. I'm only going to collect my sister from the station.'

'I'm afraid we have urgent business in town, Mrs Twilling,' said Campbell. 'Burt,' he said to the tractor driver, 'Could you back up to that gateway.' Campbell pointed to a field entrance behind the tractor. The tractor driver grunted. It sounded like a reluctant, but relieved, consent. As he moved the tractor Campbell took the driver's seat of the Rolls Royce and lurched it towards a muddy gateway on the opposite side from the one the tractor was in. This road was low lying and the soil was thick, fertile and wet. He was tempted to leave the car there so he could watch Mrs Twilling's kid shod feet pick their way through the mud, but he didn't.

He didn't have time. He feared, because he had been too slow at catching the murderer, another slaughtering had taken place and he had to get to the crime scene. He felt as if he ought to be able to smell the murderer from the crime. He waved Parnold through and then drove Mrs Twilling's car back onto the road. With his own feet quite dry he settled back again in his passenger seat while Parnold stabbed at the accelerator and swore about Mrs Twilling.

Parnold even suggested that she might have blocked the road on purpose to delay them. Campbell agreed that it was always a possibility, but he made it sound more like a gross impossibility. This road would bring them into Ouse Crossing close to the railway station, whereas the main road through the forest would take them to the far side of town during the rush hour.

A group of police cars had gathered outside the Fenman's house. They were all neatly parked along the kerbside, most were empty. Campbell walked past them and made for the front door. He found Mrs Fenman seated in the living room examining her lap. The only other occupant was WPC Garden who was standing next to the radiator opposite Mrs Fenman.

Campbell felt he'd assessed the atmosphere and was about to speak when he heard Parnold's voice say, 'Mrs Fenman, is your husband here?'

'No, he's not,' she replied. The words were steady and without defiance.

Campbell meant, but failed, to give Parnold a withering glance for his sharply spoken question. But it had given him two answers. The body was not her husband's and Mr Fenman was not there. He watched Parnold show her the torch. It affected Catherine Fenman badly, what colour was left in her face disappeared. Her eyes ogled the object as she muttered,

'It's like ours.' She touched it. 'There should've been one in the boot, and a tow rope. The switch was taped up on ours.' She rubbed her finger over the electrical tape. 'In the forest I could feel the tape. I didn't think anything of it. The torch was all slippery...'

Now that the inspector and his sergeant were looking at the shed, Catherine was looking for her daughters. She'd been horrified when she'd seen the back garden crawling with blue and white over-alled strangers. The wheelbarrow had been moved away from the gate to let in people carrying plastic bags. She'd turned away from the back door when a large plastic bag holding Kelvin's body had been wheeled away. She didn't love him, but she wanted his life back inside him. She wanted him to live and Robert back.

Robert had to be here to tell them he hadn't murdered anyone. The torch confirmed his innocence. To leave his own torch at the murder was stupid. Robert was not stupid.

In the living room she found Molly and Laura. They were giving, unprompted, two policewomen their own version of the morning's happenings. Molly was bouncing on the edge of her seat and saying, 'Mum got blood all over her feet. It was disgusting.' Catherine started to slither back out of the room while Laura told Molly to be quiet. One of the policewomen followed her from the room. Catherine recognised her, with her brown curls and freckled nose, as the one from the hospital. She acknowledged this with a nod and sat on the stairs. Then she sank her face in her hands and started to cry. She felt WPC Garden sit on the step below her. There wasn't room to sit next to each other.

'I'm sorry,' said Catherine referring to her tears. 'Why me? Why should I find these bodies? It seems so unfair: first Mr Twilling and now Kelvin.'

Catherine noticed the policewoman's eyebrows twitch. She knew she'd registered the use of Kelvin's first name. 'It's no secret,' she continued, relieved to confess. 'We had been lovers, but not for a while. Perhaps it was out of boredom. I don't know. It never seemed real. He'd always seemed artificial.' She shook her head. 'That seems callous now. No-one deserves to die like that.'

Campbell had seen enough. It seemed to him that the smell of blood affected his sinuses. He blew into a large white handkerchief. Tilting his head sideways he looked up to Parnold. The body had been taken down from the rafters and was being zipped into a body bag, but the camera was still flashing as the evidence collectors moved about him. He seemed to be the only stationary person in the already cordoned off area. The hook and rope with the knots intact, from which the body had been hanging, were removed carefully as before, placed in a plastic bag, labelled and the details recorded in a book. He felt for a moment like asking the white overalled scrapers and dusters if they knew who did it. He stopped himself as he heard a similar quip come from Jenner. He closed his eyes to shut out the activities around him. He tried to shut out the noise. He envisaged the corpse hanging as it had been when he first arrived at the scene. It was identical to that of Frederick Twilling.

Parnold had recognised the body as Frederick Twilling's solicitor, Kelvin Silverton. Campbell walked back from the garden into the kitchen with his sergeant two paces behind him. He stood still. He could hear Mrs Fenman talking on the stairs. When she stopped he moved forwards, and gently checked his information, 'What was Kelvin's surname, Mrs Fenman?'

'Kelvin Silverton. At first he was just our solicitor,' she replied. Her eyes were shiny and blood shot from the tears, but he could see she was not going to cry again.

'Mrs Fenman, where is your husband?' asked Campbell making the words sound like a Scottish lullaby.

'I don't know. He left the hospital. He changed his clothes. I found them in the bathroom. He must have come in the back way because he hadn't picked up the post. He must have gone out that way too and gone back to the hospital. We must have missed each other.' Mrs Fenman looked at him. Her eyes were imploring him to believe her.

'How would he'ave got here from the hospital? We have his car and bike for forensic examination?' asked Parnold.

Campbell watched Mrs Fenman's face turn towards Parnold and her expression change. He was amused to see her guard her contempt with politeness, 'We are only minutes from the hospital. He would have walked as I did last night.'

'Going back to last night, Mrs Fenman, did you hear any strange noises?' asked Campbell.

'No, nothing at all. The girls slept with me, in my room, at the front of the house. I didn't sleep well, but I didn't hear anything unusual.'

'What about earlier? What were your movements after leaving the hospital, Mrs Fenman?' Campbell hunched his shoulders and listened intently.

'I went straight round to Sadie, Sadie Groom. She's been looking after the children. I picked them up. I was there about half an hour. It was about nine o'clock by the time I got home,' she replied. Campbell saw something behind Mrs Fenman's eyes flicker.

'And?' asked Campbell. He caught Parnold's look of confusion. He knew his colleague had not seen her near movement and her sentence had been complete, her words had not faltered. He knew there was something she was not telling them.

'That's it. That's all that happened,' she said and Campbell felt shut out.

'Mrs Fenman, your husband had motives for killing both these men. One had accused him of assaulting him and could ruin his career. The other one had been your lover. You must be able to see that for yourself. And now your husband has disappeared. Mrs Fenman, we need to have a look around your house.' Campbell was shuffling his feet and rubbing his hands together. 'It's not too warm in here,' he added conversationally.

'People keep opening the doors,' said Mrs Fenman flatly. 'Yes, of course you can look round. I know my husband didn't do these horrible murders. He couldn't have. He found Frederick Twilling with me.'

'Mrs Fenman, he could have arranged it that way. And you didn't know where he was during the time Kelvin Silverton was killed.' Campbell squatted down opposite her, his eyes level with hers. 'From what you've said there could be some risk to your-self. It may be that the murderer wants you to find the bodies.' He had to tell her more, so she might open up. 'Mrs Fenman, did you know your husband had a meeting with Mr Frederick Twilling on the morning of his murder?'

'No, but I saw Mr Twilling at lunch time when I went to get the car from Robert. Mr Twilling was with Mercer, my husband's boss and another man.'

'Thank you, Mrs Fenman,' said Campbell, noticing that she was looking firmly at the hall carpet as she spoke. There was something that happened outside the Town Hall she was not telling him about. He let it go for now as this third man sounded interesting. 'We have witnesses who can tell us that Mr Frederick Twilling was alive and well up until six thirty on the night he was murdered. But, perhaps, you could describe this other man.'

'He was tall, grey, middle to late forties. He was wearing a brown suit and soft brown shoes.'

'Anything else, Mrs Fenman?'

'Yes, a mole on the top of his head, on his bald patch.'

'Thank you, Mrs Fenman.' Campbell looked around him at the trampled house. 'Have you someone you can stay with?'

'I'm going to Sadie's,' she said. 'My husband is innocent, Inspector,' she added. Her eyes were hungry for the reassurance Campbell knew he couldn't give her.

'WPC Garden will escort you,' he said. How was this woman connected to these murders, he wondered? Was she an intended victim or an accomplice, or was she on the edge of it all involved in only finding the bodies? This madness was happening too quickly. There seemed no time to stand back and analyse it properly. How was he going to stop it?

He moved out of the front door into the front garden, and it seemed warmer here than in the house.

Parnold thought Campbell seemed to be doing some sort of exercise. He was standing with his feet apart, his hands clasped behind his back and he was breathing deeply. With each breath he put his weight onto the balls of his feet. As he let out his breath he lowered his heels back to the ground. His long thin limbs were occupying the width of the path and completely blocking the Fenman's front gate. Parnold felt trapped in the Fenman's small front garden.

'Don't you think Catherine Fenman oughtn't stay with Sadie Groom?' asked Parnold. 'That woman could well be involved with Robert Fenman.'

'Threads from a rag,' said Campbell rocking back on his heels.

Parnold frowned, what was Campbell on about? 'She could go to her mother's,' he suggested.

'Would you go to your mother's?'

''Course I would.'

'I don't think I would,' said Campbell. 'Let her go to her friend's we have no evidence against Sadie Groom.' Parnold wanted to object but Campbell said, 'You spoke to Kelvin Silverton yesterday to check Jonathan Twilling's alibi?' Campbell made the suggestion standing on tiptoe.

'Yes, Sir,' said Parnold. He felt himself redden. 'He was quite alive when I spoke to him.'

'I'm not accusing you, Parnold.'

Parnold looked at Campbell carefully, but he couldn't detect a smile on the Inspector's face. Parnold was having difficulty keeping his temper in check. Campbell was irritating in the extreme. But his reputation for solving crimes was well known and to be respected.

'Did Silverton confirm Jonathan Twilling's statement?' Campbell asked after a moment during which he breathed out and lowered his heels to the path.

'Yes, Sir.'

'Good.' At last Campbell moved from the gateway. Parnold rushed through and gained the driver's seat before Campbell had reached the car and felt calmer.

'How was your bicycle ride yesterday?' Campbell asked apparently finding the passenger seat to his liking.

'It was alright,' said Parnold. He'd told him yesterday it fitted into their view of events, for goodness sake.

'Robert Fenman said he left home at seven fifteen. It took me half an hour to bike from his house to the woods. That ties in with Mrs Fenman seeing him at seven forty five when she got out of the car for the can of petrol.'

'Good. But if, as you think, Robert Fenman was the culprit and his wife a possible accomplice that part of their story would certainly tally.' Campbell looked relaxed. 'Perhaps, Robert Fenman hired a car, put his bicycle in the back, picked up Twilling brought him down that back lane and took him to his gantry and murdered him,' suggested Campbell.

'That's a possibility,' said Parnold eagerly. 'I'll check out all the hire firms and their cars.'

'And we must put out a search for Robert Fenman. All the usuals: pictures in the press, railway stations etcetera.'

Parnold said, 'Yes Sir.'

'Oh, and while you're at it, could you check out Jonathan and Sarah Twilling. It would be interesting to know what the wife and son of

Frederick Twilling – our first murder victim – were doing last night.' Campbell paused for a moment. 'And get a list from Jonathan Twilling of all the people his father swindled.' He got out of the car. Parnold saw satisfaction in Campbell's movements. He felt it was from snowing him under with work.

# Chapter 7

Campbell lengthened his stride across the police station car park. He always tried to look efficient around the building, but it was his least favourite location. If he'd wanted an office job he'd been an accountant, he'd told Margaret on more than one occasion. He loathed paper work and being caught by telephone calls in the middle of thinking matters through. He toyed with the idea of borrowing someone else's office so he would be more difficult to find but every other office seemed to be occupied so it looked as though he would have to use his own. He looked inside it. His desk was strewn with paper. He closed the door without going in.

'You,' he addressed a WPC at a computer screen whose blond hair was scraped back into a neat pleat. 'Could you get the statements from my desk, the ones the slaughter men gave us, please?'

She looked at him oddly. "Must be new", thought Campbell. While she was fetching the papers he rummaged in his pockets for his spare key to Parnold's car. Parnold would have vacated it by now to gather the man-power for the latest tasks he had been set.

Turning the pages of their statements in the car, Campbell found the slaughter men offered no leads on the enquiry. Indeed, most of the slaughterhouse workers had been at the get together at the Compass public house on the market place on the night of the Frederick Twilling murder. They had started early and were there until late. Then they were observed by two of the local constables, some being taxied and others staggering home. Campbell marvelled at Parnold's efficiency in getting statements from the taxi drivers too, but by that time Frederick Twilling had been dead some hours. Of the half dozen who hadn't attended from the slaughterhouse: two were on holiday; three were at home with friends and family; and one was in hospital with kidney stones.

Four slaughter men had recently changed jobs. Two of these were at the get together and the other two had moved out of the area. Parnold had tracked them down, however, and they had been visited by their local constabulary. They had been vouched for by their families and new places of work. Most of the local vets had been visited already and could be accounted for by their customers or families.

His thoughts flipped back to his dream. It pleased him that his mind worked even while he slept and made links that his conscious mind was not capable of. He remembered there were other people he'd seen jostling in the bus queue, people he couldn't see properly. Then there was what Mrs Fenman had told him at the hospital. She'd said she'd seen another man with Mercer and Frederick Twilling on the day of the first murder. A man with a mole on the top of his head. Campbell rolled out of the car and back into the office.

He looked hopefully at the first police constable he came across in the outer office. He recognised her as the one he'd sent for the reports on the slaughter men.

She gave her name with a smile, 'WPC Jenner, Sir.'

'You were at the murder site?'

'Yes, Sir. Hands in pockets, Sir?'

'Aye, quite so,' said Campbell. 'Do you know where Mercer is at the moment? You know, Fenman's boss at Ouseland District Council.'

She accepted this request tilting her head to the side and she replied, 'No, Sir, but I can find out.' Campbell noticed the crispness in her voice, but it didn't tie in with the laughter in her eyes.

He found his office and sidled up to his desk. On the top was the pathologist's report on Frederick Twilling. When WPC Jenner returned, he immediately complained that he had not been told about its arrival. There was no reply from the WPC, just those eyes smiling at him.

Looking back at the report, he immediately forgot Jenner's presence. 'Twilling was drugged,' he said out loud. 'And the chances are Silverton was too, that's why no-one heard anything. I should have worked that one out for myself.'

He heard Jenner clear her throat. He looked at her questioningly.

'Mr Mercer is taking a few days off, Sir,' she replied. 'Here's his address.'

'Thank you, Constable,' said Campbell with humble politeness. WPC Jenner broke into a smile, but Campbell's, 'Get Parnold for me, please,' made her face mend rapidly, and she left the room.

When Parnold came in, Campbell directed him to, 'Find out all the pharmacists, doctors and anaesthetists who might have had access to this drug.' He handed him a piece of paper with the chemical name spelt out in large letters for him. 'We also need to know if there have been any thefts from these places.' Jenner knocked and came in before he could say any more and handed him a report which had just arrived from the forensic laboratory.

Campbell assumed the tasks he'd given Parnold would keep him and his team busy, so he walked out into the outer office and picked out WPC Jenner. He asked her to go with him.

He felt her treading in his footsteps as they walked across the car park so he ordered her to walk beside him. She seemed to stoop as if embarrassed. 'I'm a human being, WPC Jenner, not a wolf. My canine leanings are only in following the scent, because it takes a human to do this job.'

Jenner straightened, smiled nervously and seemed to adjust rapidly to her new role.

Campbell again used his key to gain access to Parnold's car and he drove himself and Jenner out of the yard. Cars never felt part of him. They always seemed to be his adversary. He could pull the blasted things to bits and understand every working part, but he had difficulty driving. He would have liked to have been able to live life without ever having to use one, but the work required it. And he had concluded that was the case for everyone else living in the countryside away from the limited bus routes. So he sat tensely over the wheel as he drove out onto Hillvill Road.

Mercer lived out on the Hillvill road, two miles beyond the forest where Twilling was murdered. The line of fields was broken by a hamlet consisting of six houses and a disused church. Jenner pointed it out and then the opening to a track. They pulled up this muddy lane and stopped by Mercer's cottage. Beyond, the lane twisted its way around the edge of fields into the distance. Mercer's cottage was made of flint. Each piece had been divided by craftsman three hundred years before to give a smooth, shining grey surface to every stone. The cottage stood on its own, but from its length Campbell could see that when it was built it had been several homes, now it was one. Its small front windows were divided into many diamond shaped panes and they peeped out over the fields to the west, back towards the forest of Frederick Twilling's murder.

There was a movement by one of these windows followed shortly afterwards by the front door opening. Mercer came out to the garden gate clad in brown cords and green wellingtons with a body warmer over a thick beige jumper. He sounded false with his over friendly greeting, to which Campbell replied,

'Good morning, Sir. I wonder if you could give me your movements for last night?'

'Last night? Twilling was murdered the night before. What's all this about?' Mercer replied, opening the gate to let Jenner and Campbell in the garden. His movements were stiff. He was already guarding his thoughts.

'If you could just tell me, Sir? It would be a great help,' said Campbell.

'Yesterday evening I visited my mother in hospital in town until seven-thirty.' Mercer was watching WPC Jenner.

'Ouse Crossing?' asked Campbell. Mercer nodded and said that was right. Campbell couldn't bring himself to like the way Mercer spoke. He decided that the pulling at his 'i's and 'e's was probably an affectation to hide an accent. 'Mr Mercer, what did you do after that?' added Campbell.

'I got some fish and chips and came home.' Mercer's face was beginning to look defiant.

'Were you alone?' asked Campbell.

'No, my wife was with me. She's a nurse. I waited in the hospital for her after visiting hours so we could go to the chip shop. Then we came home together.' Mercer's cheeks and the end of his nose became flushed as he spoke.

'Did anyone see you while you waited for your wife?'

'I don't know. I expect so. I waited in the foyer. There are some seats there. I expect the receptionists can vouch for me.' Mercer's hands twitched. 'Look, what is all this, Inspector? And why have you brought your girl-friend along?'

Campbell smiled, ignoring the rudeness of the question. He was convinced most rudeness disappeared if confronted with pleasant politeness. 'I'm sorry. I should have introduced you to my colleague, WPC Jenner.' He nodded at the pair to force them to shake hands. They did so. Campbell thanked Mercer and told him that he would probably hear on the lunch time news that Kelvin Silverton had been murdered, adding: 'Did you know him?'

'Yes, vaguely. He was Twilling's solicitor. He was young and brash. I didn't like him,' said Mercer. Campbell raised his eyebrows, and Mercer's colour rose some more. 'I didn't kill him,' Mercer said loudly.

The man was on edge, Campbell calculated that he would be able to see whether he was lying or telling the truth in this state, so he posed the question, 'There was a man with you and Frederick Twilling at lunch time on the day that gentleman was murdered. Who was this other man?'

'I met him once before at a party given by Frederick Twilling,' said Donald Mercer. 'I didn't really socialise with Twilling. He invited everyone to these occasions. A free drink and some good food. There were no conditions attached to it. No corruption.'

Campbell was beginning to feel cold. 'The thought of corruption came readily to your mind. But I am interested in murders, Mr Mercer. At this moment I'm only interested in corruption if it has a bearing on the case. Does it?'

Mercer sighed. Some of his face colour left him. 'Look, Inspector, this chap, his name was Reede. I don't know where he came from or anything about him. He was a really shifty chap. I didn't like him.'

'Thank you,' said Campbell jotting the name down in his note book. 'I'm getting chilled out here, and, I expect, you are too. Good day to you.' Nodding to WPC Jenner to get in the passenger seat, he got in the driver's seat and turned the engine on. As they drove away they left Mercer staring fixedly at the ploughed fields in front of his home.

'He's up to his ears in something,' said Jenner.

'Aye, but is it murder?' asked Campbell. Was this Council official the sort of person to carry out two murders, he wondered. The man's wife worked at the hospital and could have got the drugs. But could he have the mind to calculate and execute that sort of crime? Mercer had, after all, taunted Campbell about catching the right murderer. He claimed to have an alibi, and, anyway, how could he know about slaughtering?

The murderer, whoever it was, had killed a second time, Campbell was sure that person had got pleasure out of it. There was still hate in the cuts, a controlled hate. It dug at Campbell's inner fears, at past terrors hidden by adulthood. He remembered the first time the full horror of war had come to him. He had been ten years old when he had understood that guns and bombs killed and that people had weapons which could kill every living thing. He had always wanted to prevent war, but he had been powerless. Surely that was why he had become a catcher of criminals, an attempt to stop a small part of the killing.

And this murderer was at war with life. Campbell knew he had been dragged into the war zone. The Inspector flexed his shoulders to hide the shiver that escaped from his spine. He knew he had to catch the slaughterer before this war destroyed anyone else.

It almost overcame Campbell's reasoning. But he knew he had to keep thinking, working at the puzzle. He looked across at the church.

Momentarily he was back at Campbell's Castle among the stones, big flat hewn stones not like the flints embedded in the mortar of the small building opposite him. Tight narrow winding tower steps filled his mind, confusing his direction. His breath shortened with every step taken upwards, taking oxygen from his brain, increasing his disorientation.

'Are you all right, Sir,' enquired Jenner.

'Round tower to the church, Jenner -- very particular to the area.'

'Yes, Sir,' said Jenner.

Jenner looked out of the window and back at him. He caught her "What are you talking about" look, and then turned his mind to solving the crime. He would go back to the scene of Frederick Twilling's murder. He had to see it the way the murderer and the victim saw it, not as he, a policeman, had seen it.

# Chapter 8

Catherine didn't want an escort. WPC Garden wasn't unpleasant, even if she was a bit scruffy for a policewoman. At least she walked a discrete two paces behind. It was just that she wanted to tell Sadie herself about Kelvin's death, quietly, unobserved. She also felt the police looked at her with suspicion. She somehow managed to hold on to Laura and Molly's hands as she turned the corner and looked across at Sadie's house with a suitcase wheeling behind her and the second smaller case balanced on top. Garden had offered to help, but she didn't want her help.

Sadie's was less inviting this morning, but what was behind her was worse. She tried to convince herself that Kelvin had never been a real person to her, so why should she fear his corpse? But she did and he had been real.

Sadie let them in without asking questions. Catherine did not manage to speak to her friend before WPC Garden took Sadie into the front room and closed the door. They would be talking about Kelvin. Catherine had seen something in her friend's face as she went through the door which made her feel Sadie would not be the confidante she'd been the day before.

She reached for Sadie's phone. She knew that she would not be denied such a simple favour.

Before she lifted the receiver she directed Molly and Laura to go upstairs and to take the bags with them. Molly bumped the smallest bag up behind her while Laura collected the larger one. Catherine noted how neither of them looked anything like Evelyn and hoped they would never behave like her. Then she dialled her mother's number.

She can't make me stay with her, thought Catherine. She closed her eyes and saw the flat black fields of the fens spreading out below her childhood home:

Once, the remains of scorched wheat stems would have stood there in irregularly blackened rows. Now the stubble would be poking irregularly through the turned earth and she remembered how, as a child, she'd stood close to a field while the farmer burnt the straw. The heat waves buffeted her as the flames were pulled up into a static tornado. She remembered her panic. Today the fields were quiet and serene. Today the landscape was contrary to the state of her life.

The wind blew through the window. She was cold. "I'm already at Sadie's. It will be easy to talk to her now. It's never easy," she corrected herself. The phone burred in short ringing phrases in her ear until her mother's voice barked at her.

'Evelyn, please listen,' Catherine pleaded, but Evelyn wouldn't. There was a tirade of abuse about Robert.

'Robert's missing.' Catherine closed her eyes, seeing her husband in her imagination, wanting him to be the one she was talking to, not her mother. The older woman at the other end of the line did not stop talking. 'Please, Evelyn,' she interrupted, 'Kelvin's dead.' Her mother became silent. Catherine tried to calculate her mother's reaction. Evelyn had met Kelvin on several occasions, but had never shown any particular interest in him until recently when it seemed she thought him preferable to Robert.

'I can't come and see you,' said Evelyn.

'What?' said Catherine, reeling from the change of direction. She hadn't even suggested it. She would never suggest it. 'That's OK, Evelyn,' she said, and she knew she said it with too much relief.

'No, it's not OK. I haven't got a car. Both George's and mine have broken down. We are quite stranded here. You will have to come and see me,' said Evelyn.

It struck Catherine as bizarre that both cars should be out of order. She thought this might be one of her mother's attention seeking devices. 'I can't, Evelyn. Not today. I'll come and see you tomorrow. The police have my car, but I should think Sadie will lend me hers.'

At that moment Sadie and WPC Garden came from the front room and Sadie opened the front door. She let the policewoman out and reclosed it. Catherine watched. She thought her friend seemed too keen to get rid of the uniformed woman. They caught each other's eyes, both changed them to neutrality and Sadie nodded her agreement at the loan of her car.

Having been told of the loan of the car Evelyn seemed pacified and

Catherine found herself able to say 'Goodbye' with only a slight feeling of reasonless guilt, but with a greater dread of the proposed visit.

Campbell drove in the same jolting slow manner away from Mercer's as he'd arrived. He wasn't consciously driving; he was watching the forest rising up from the ground on his right hand side.

The variety of scenery in his district pleased him. Here were the rolling chalk hills with their soft wood forests, crops of wheat and sweet corn. To the north was the coast and to the east and south lay the black fens with their sinking soil and high banked rivers.

The blank wall of pine trees staring at the black poplars that edged the fields on his left brought Campbell back to Catherine Fenman. She had come this way the night of the murder of Frederick Twilling. There was nothing unusual in that. This was the most direct route from Hillvill to Ouse Crossing. He passed several roadways that cut through the forest forming it into a grid, each section being a large field of trees. These would, he knew, be harvested together.

'This is the one,' he said to Jenner, who was sitting quietly in the passenger seat. He slowed the unmarked police car on the road, irritating a speeding motorist who beeped loudly at the inconvenience. Campbell looked at the disappearing vehicle, but he had no interest in it. He indicated right and went down the lane, which was thought to have been used by the murderer. He stopped the car and, without warning, swung out of the door and plunged into the forest.

When Jenner reached him he had already been squatting on the pine needled floor, not far from where the body had been found, for several moments. He looked up at her. 'The murderer must have been covered with blood,' he said to her still looking at the ground. 'Frederick Twilling had been killed only moments before Catherine Fenman had found him, yet a comprehensive search of the forest found no discarded bloodied clothes or murder weapon.' He sighed and pulled out of his pocket Mary Brown's initial forensic report. After a moment he gasped, 'It's a wheelbarrow. Of course.'

'What, Sir?' enquired Jenner.

'The murderer got the drugged victim through the forest in a wheelbarrow not a trailer. That's what that tyre print was from. A trailer would have been difficult to handle through the trees and the car would need a tow bar. None of the suspects' cars have such a thing.' He looked up. 'So, not a trailer. That means that the car would have had to have been big enough to get a wheelbarrow in it and if Fenman did it, his cycle too.'

'Most cars can these days with the back seats down, Sir,' said Jenner, 'or with a bike rack fitted.'

'All the same, Parnold must be informed. You'd better go back to the car and tell him.' He watched her go. She was about Mrs Fenman's build. She was not lean but being ten years younger gave her a softness in her shape that was lost to Catherine Fenman. He guessed that both women would be strong enough to move a heavily laden wheelbarrow if they wanted to. The last thought provoked a memory from the recent past. He too would have to use the car radio.

When he reached the car Jenner had just finished talking to Parnold. Her face was pinched by the cold air and she seemed relieved to be back in the warmth of the car. He took the radio and asked to be put through to Mary Brown. The scientist sounded pleased to hear from him, but he knew that was a pleasure which she showed for everyone. Before he could reply to her greeting she continued, 'I know what you're going to ask me. Yes, we've got the Fenman's wheelbarrow, and we're making checks on it now. And, yes, I'll let you have the results as soon as possible, Campbell.'

Campbell caught Jenner's mouth twitch in the start of an amused smile. 'Forensic may be a major source of information, but we catch the murderers and thieves,' he said, failing to stop her mouth from forming a broad smile. He thought he ought to tell her that the police don't smile outwardly and stopped because he had caught the humour. As if infected by some alien disease his face smiled by itself.

'We must look at the timetable.' He realigned his face. 'Who could have come up here shortly before or at the same time as Catherine Fenman broke down? Someone came here to meet and to kill Frederick Twilling. It was planned. There was a gantry. On my walk yesterday I only just managed to get here from Jonathan Twilling's house in the same amount of time as Twilling Senior would have needed to get here. You have to allow ten to fifteen minutes for him to be drugged and killed. That was about the length of time Mrs Fenman was sitting in her car too frightened and dizzy to get out. '

'There has to be a reason behind the two murders, a common motive. We can't look at each on its own, surely?' asked Jenner.

'First we look at them individually, gathering evidence from each incident. If they overlap, as these appear to do. We must look at the ways in which they overlap, but we cannot heap them together to work them out, Jenner. We must also look carefully at the differences.

'Now, let's consider some of the overlaps. The victims were connected through business with Mercer and Jonathan Twilling. Catherine Fenman found both bodies. Robert Fenman had reason to dislike Silverton for his involvement with his wife and Frederick Twilling for his alleged sharp practices.'

'Robert Fenman is missing,' said Jenner, raising her right eyebrow.

'That may or may not be connected. And, the possibilities are that he's been abducted, he's run away out of fear or guilt, or he has also been murdered, but has not been found yet.' Campbell looked at Jenner. He needed to talk out the possibilities and she listened with enthusiasm. 'If the Fenmans had done it together and lied about the timing they could have carried it out. There was a long time between the Fenmans finding the body and them contacting the police. They explained this by saying that they tried their mobile phones but there was no reception here.'

'I tried my phone. It's the same network as their's and it didn't work.'

'Did Robert Fenman have a work phone?'

'Yes. It was on the same network.'

'Right. So, Catherine Fenman would not be left so her husband had carried her to the cottage down the road where they said they had trouble gaining access to the phone because of their bloody appearance.' He shuffled through his note book. 'Here's the address. I made a note to go and see them. I didn't find the statement from the owner, Mr Middleton, at all in keeping with my timetable.'

Campbell started the car. Low sunshine was streaming into the interior warming his back and catching the rear view mirror. His foot slipped off the clutch and they lurched forwards. Jenner offered to drive but he ignored her. When they reached the road Jenner observed out loud that the track continued on the other side of the main road into the fields beyond the black poplars. Again Campbell ignored her as he gained a space for the car on the main road. Half a mile further along they passed the junction on the left which led up to Sarah and Jonathan Twilling's homes. The same distance again brought them to the Middleton's cottage.

Looking at his notebook again, Campbell said, 'Mrs Irene Middleton?' as the door opened to him.

The woman sighed. 'If I see another policeman I'll go spare,' she said, and then she added accusingly, 'You're not local.' Irene Middleton was dressed in slippers and socks which sagged around her thick, stockinged legs. Her full gathered skirt draped unevenly about her overly-large hips. Her expansive bosom seemed to be supported by her arms folded beneath it. Her cheeks wobbled as she spoke.

'No, I'm not,' agreed Campbell, 'but I am a policeman: Inspector Campbell.' WPC Jenner came up behind him and shuffled her feet until he introduced her.

'You don't look local either,' complained Irene Middleton.

Jenner did not reply.

Campbell started to chat. First he commented on the weather and, after that, he asked how she was coping with all the excitement the murder had brought to her door. Lastly, he came back to the events of the night Frederick Twilling was murdered.

'I've already told one of your men what happened. We saw nothing. My husband sat over there watching the telly.' She pointed to an easy chair between the window and the fireplace. Its back was facing the window. The only comfortable place to look was the television screen. 'I saw them first. I was sitting here.' She pointed to a dining table stood by the wall with three chairs around it. The fourth chair was to the side of the kitchen doorway. 'We don't have a dining room, but I like to sit up the table and do a bit of sewing while Harry watches telly.' She leaned forward and touched WPC Jenner on the arm and said, 'I thought I'd seen a pair of ghosts.'

'What do you mean by "seen"?' asked Campbell,

'They were up the window,' explained Irene Middleton.

'But it was dark. Don't you normally close your curtains?' asked Campbell.

'Not regular, only when the wind comes that way. Then it's stingy in here and we shut the curtains to keep out the cold. My husband, Harry, says he likes to see the night. But I don't know how he can sittin' there.' She pointed to his television chair.

'What time was it?' asked Campbell.

'Harry was watching a quiz show and I was stitching this fire screen. It must have been eight fifteen, eight twenty. That clock's a bit slow up there.' Irene Middleton pointed to a sturdy wooden framed clock hanging above the mantel piece.

'Mrs Middleton, the Fenman's call was not recorded on the emergency number until eight thirty,' explained Campbell. 'You left them standing out there for fifteen minutes. That isn't what you told our people earlier, Mrs

Middleton.'

'They were all covered in blood. I screamed and told them to go away. They weren't going to murder me. They put their hands up to show they were empty, but I sent Harry for his shot gun all the same.' Irene Middleton was looking at Campbell for approval. He said nothing, he just glared at her. 'We let them in the front door and the woman collapsed,' she continued. 'We wrapped her in a blanket. Your lab people took it. They will bring it back?'

'You should have phoned the police yourselves if you were too frightened to let them in, Mrs Middleton. You were quite wrong to point a gun at them,' said Campbell.

'What about my blanket?' asked Irene Middleton again. Campbell was unmoved by her sixty year old face pulled into a pout.

'Have you a receipt for it, Mrs Middleton?' asked Campbell.

'That's a bit of paper, not a blanket,' observed Mrs Middleton.

Campbell changed the subject, 'How did they appear to you?'

'I told you, like ghosts,' said Mrs Middleton, again touching WPC Jenner on the arm.

'Their emotional state, how did you see that? Were they different? Was one behaving in one way and the other in another?' asked Campbell.

Mrs Middleton paused. 'I told you the woman collapsed. The man made the phone call. He looked and sounded scared. His eyes were bulging.'

'So would mine be if I'd just seen a murdered body, carried my wife over a mile and had a shot gun pointed at me,' said WPC Jenner. Campbell could see Mrs Middleton was annoying her. He was going to ask Irene Middleton another question when there was a knock at the door.

'Come in, lovie,' called Mrs Middleton. The door opened. It was filled by a large man in a white overall. He was carrying a basket with a selection of creamy white parcels tied with string and wearing a large apron with thin white stripes going across a dark blue back ground.

'Hello, Mum,' said the man kissing Irene Middleton on the cheek. The same heavy features were proof of their relationship.

'This is my son, Mark, Inspector. He's a butcher. He comes this way on his delivery round. He doesn't own the business, you understand. But he's a good boy. I expect he'll manage the shop one of these days.'

'Which shop is that?' asked Campbell.

'Waverley's of Ouse Crossing. They're in the High Street,' replied Mark Middleton.

'The meat is beautiful from there,' said his mother.

'They used to kill their own meat, but with all the regulations and such like they don't anymore,' said Mark Middleton, spreading out his large chest by flexing his shoulders back.

'Thank you. Thank you very much.' The words 'BUTCHERS' and 'WAVERLEY'S' went down in Campbell's book. He squeezed his slender frame past the large butcher to find the air outside refreshing and stimulating. He breathed it deeply while he waited for Jenner to escape from Mrs Middleton who was again asking about her blanket.

When he contacted the office on the car radio he found all his staff involved in the list of jobs he'd given Parnold. Campbell leaned back in the driver's seat and stretched his legs. This job he could do himself and from the comfort of his own home. WPC Jenner fidgeted in the passenger seat.

'Don't you think there might be more murders, Sir?' she asked. 'We've already had two in nearly the same number of days. It's obvious there's a madman loose, and Mr Fenman is missing. Shouldn't we be doing more to find him?'

'We're doing everything we need to do in that line,' said Campbell. 'After all, he is only one of the suspects.' He was going to be calm. Only in that way could he conduct this investigation evenly. He wanted to judge each personality and motive only speeded, not panicked, by the fear of another murder.

'Would you like a coffee?' he asked her brightly. The young woman blushed and nodded. He couldn't read what this meant and so he just turned the car round, drove half a mile up the road and took the right T-junction, which went past Jonathan Twilling's house. Several miles further on the road ended in another T-junction and Campbell turned left onto a byroad. If he'd turned right they'd have been on the back road into Ouse Crossing, the one on which Campbell and Parnold had been stopped by Mrs Twilling's Rolls Royce and the tractor. Instead, a couple of sweeping bends later the car passed around a large oak tree and crunched down the lane leading to his cottage.

He found Margaret sewing in the dining room. He wasn't sure whose idea it had been for her to work from home, but he found it most convenient with his strange hours. It meant they saw each other sometimes. The only problem as far as he could see was that she never seemed to stop.

Going into the kitchen, Campbell spotted some soup on the stove, so he turned on the heat with his right hand to warm it up. With his left hand he lifted the phone directory from the shelf and started thumbing the pages for 'butchers'. He passed it to WPC Jenner with instructions to list all the butchers within a fifty mile radius of Ouse Crossing.

A few moments later, Margaret came in and looked at Jenner's list.

'I'm after butchers that used to kill their own meat,' explained Campbell.

'There must be quite a few people with that sort of knowledge,' observed Margaret turning down the soup. Campbell was aware of Margaret offering WPC Jenner a cup of coffee and asking the policewoman her name. He thought he heard the girl reply that it was Bridget.

'I was keeping an eye on that,' complained Campbell looking over his wife's shoulder at the soup, while she scraped the noodles off the bottom of the pan. He got an, 'I can see that,' so he went back over to the kitchen table and Jenner's list.

'This directory doesn't cover the whole area,' said Bridget Jenner.

'I've got an old one for the east of the region on top of my filing cabinet in the dining room. We just come outside the area for Ouse Crossing here,' said Margaret dishing up the soup. Campbell heard his wife offer Jenner some of the soup and ask her if she could baby sit their nearly grown children for them tonight. He didn't hear the reply but Margaret looked pleased when she joined him in the dining room.

'It's five years old,' grumbled Campbell, pointing to the pages of the directory made yellow with age.

'You can always look it up on the internet,' said Margaret.

'This'll do for now.' He took it into the kitchen while Margaret returned to her piles of fabric and tissue paper. He dumped his book next to his soup and examined its pages while he supped the bowl's scolding contents.

His spoon splashed into his bowl. 'Hah,' he said. The exclamation was full of satisfaction and curiosity. He finished his soup and took the directory back into the dining room. He told his wife it had been very useful and tossed it on the table. Pieces of neat, hand-made paper patterns fluttered to the floor.

'Raymond, when can you look at my car? I need it tomorrow,' he heard Margaret call as he reached the back door where Jenner was already waiting for him. He said nothing. He hadn't time to reply. He had found another piece of information, like a piece of stone from a fallen wall. He could restore the wall if he carefully placed it with the others. As soon as that wall was complete he would have the murderer so the slaughtering would stop.

He thought of Campbell's Castle and closed the door with a little unspoken sadness.

# Chapter 9

The information in the old telephone directory had changed Campbell's mind about the rest of the day. He would not have a ramble round all the butcher's shops in the area, which he'd planned after listening to Mark Middleton, when one visit may well be far more interesting.

WPC Jenner reached the car first, and offered to drive. This time he accepted. He told her where to go and watched her point Parnold's car in the direction of the Twilling's estate. She approached the entrance to the driveway along the road they'd come on earlier. Campbell flipped his and Jenner's windscreen visors down against the afternoon sun flashing through the gaps where the high clipped hedges stopped to form farm tracks. Each track was neatly shut off with a recently painted blue gate. The uniformity of the hedges and gates had a military precision. It was humanly tidy. This road always impressed Campbell.

He admitted inwardly that Jenner's driving was steady and he felt lulled. He looked out of the window feeling childhood close by. He saw the world as a brand new coin waiting for him alone to pick up. The views seemed to bounce off his retina with a sizzling freshness. He knew these feelings, they came when his investigations started to move forward.

The gatehouse belonging to Jonathan Twilling was a compromise between a cottage and a fortress, it was just two storeys, yet the roof had castellations around its copper covering. The frontage was different to Mercer's cottage, which had halved flints, in that these flints were complete round nodules. Light was given to the cottage by tall narrow windows, which were set with eight panes of glass arranged in four rows of two. The heavily timbered doors were arched and would have looked at home in a church except for their much smaller size. Lights were shining out of the windows. Campbell knew how the winter sunshine would not give enough light for detailed work in a room away from the sun. For a moment he felt sympathy for Jonathan Twilling. The young man had lost his father and his friend as well as his solicitor.

He dismissed these thoughts as Jenner jammed on the brakes. Assessing the situation, Campbell decided Jenner'd swung into the drive sharply only to find a dark blue car parked across her path. She was now swinging the steering wheel to avoid crashing into it.

She missed it as they drifted past the vehicle with order restored to continue up the drive. It could well have been the funeral director's car, but out of habit Campbell examined it in detail. It was this year's model, but not as clean as he would expect from a person in that profession. As they passed in front of the vehicle he noted its number and its dented front wing. He wrote the number on his note pad. He tilted the rear view mirror away from Jenner's driving angle so he could see behind himself without turning round. In the reflection he saw a grey haired man in his early forties being accompanied to the gate by Jonathan Twilling. Campbell could just see their top halves above the trimmed hedge.

The grey haired man was putting away a notebook in his jacket pocket. Watching the man tilt his head Campbell caught a glimpse of the front of his balding crown. The man's notebook went into his checked jacket with its leather elbow pads. He looked rural and his demeanour was relaxed. It seemed as if neither of them had seen how close Jenner had got to ploughing into the dark blue car. In fact neither of them looked at the unmarked police car making its way up the drive.

Campbell turned his attention to the front and returned the rear view mirror to the driver as the figures behind disappeared into the distance. The large country house filled the view through the windscreen.

A woman of similar height to Sarah Twilling, but of thicker build, was standing at the front door watching Campbell's car approach. When they reached her she claimed to be the widow's sister, Karen Henderson. She took Campbell and WPC Jenner through to the drawing room, assuring them that he was the first police visitor that day. 'No,' she repeated, 'Sergeant Parnold hasn't been here.' Campbell kept his concern that he was covering ground he had told Parnold to cover unspoken.

Sarah Twilling was sitting on the settee wringing her hands and sniffing. Her blotchy face and pale lips spoke silently of her grief. Her right eye had a broken blood vessel shooting across it from the physical stress of crying.

Campbell placed himself opposite her and Karen Henderson left the room closing the double doors behind her. WPC Jenner positioned herself behind Sarah Twilling, close enough to hear everything that was said.

'A strange thing happened to me today, Mrs Twilling,' said Campbell. 'I was looking in a phone directory – it must have been at least five years old. I found an entry which reminded me of our conversation yesterday. 'Petry the Butcher, Church Street, Ouse Crossing.''

'That was my first husband's business,' said Sarah Twilling in a hushed voice.

'He was a butcher, Mrs Twilling?' asked Campbell.

'Yes,' said Sarah Twilling.

Sarah Twilling was frowning in bewilderment while Jenner's eyes were smiling at the puzzle piece Campbell knew he'd been unable to get yesterday. He knew he had it now and he was going to be the one to put it in place. And it filled in a colourful corner of the picture.

'Did you know we live beside a history of slaughtering our meat?' said Sarah Twilling unprompted. 'All those charming narrow alleys and squares that we call 'Shambles' are the places where the animals were taken from the market and turned into meat.' She paused. 'What has this to do with the death of my husband, anyway?' she asked, still looking confused. Campbell ignored her question. Certain details of the murder had been with-held from the newspapers and he was not ready to release them to anyone.

'Have you any other friends or relatives who are butchers or may have worked or seen inside a slaughter house?' Campbell looked away from her. He knew people sometimes had difficulty speaking while he looked intensely into their eyes. Instead he viewed the room. It seemed the arrival of Karen Henderson had ensured standards were maintained with rugs pulled straight and cushions fluffed. Her sister, Sarah Twilling, did not look able to function on that level in her grief.

'Of course, Petry's was not originally my husband's business, Inspector. Before Harold had it, it belonged to my father, Ernest Beaver,' said Sarah Twilling. 'If you were local you might remember him. He was always winning prizes for his sausages and meat pies. My mother passed away two years before my father so when he died he left the business to me and my sister. We were both married by then. My husband was a butcher, my sister's was a builder. Karen sold her share to my husband and somewhere along the line I gave my share to him also. He wanted me to show him I trusted him.' She shuddered. 'He lost everything.'

'I've never seen a hungry butcher, Mrs Twilling,' said Campbell.

'You really don't know?' asked Sarah Twilling. 'Somehow I always think everybody knows. Yet they don't. Of course, various times haven't always been good for butchers, but it wasn't that. He was an alcoholic and a gambler, Inspector. I have to say I was relieved when he walked in front of a train.' Sarah Twilling paused. The words had been falling out of her without much strength or emotion. Now she gave a weak cough and breathed gingerly until she felt able to speak again. 'A friend of mine suggested I stand for election on the local council to take my mind off it all.' Her eyes were wet. 'You think that no-one would vote for me with that back-ground, but people have long memories around here. They remembered my father and my life before Harold Petry.'

'Your family, were they concerned for you following your marriage to Frederick Twilling?' asked Campbell. He hoped she would think of the question as gathering further background information, and allow her feelings to show.

However, she tensed as she answered, 'My sister ignores me most of the time. She never phones. If I died she would never know, unless, of course, she thought there might be something in it for her.' She lowered her voice further to say, 'That's why she's here now. Not because she cares.' Sarah Twilling let out a juddering sigh. 'My son's been worried about me though, my Ernest – not a bit like Frederick's Jonathan. I named him after my father. He didn't like Frederick, so once I became Mrs Twilling and moved here he wouldn't come and see me.'

'Is he a butcher?' asked Campbell.

'Yes. He would have had his own business too, if Harold hadn't drank and gambled it all away. He works at Waverley's in the High Street.'

Campbell wondered how he could have thought her face had looked so free of former miseries. Perhaps she was able to bring out her emotions immediately, cleanse herself and then get on with the business of living quite quickly. He couldn't believe her present state was an act.

'Did Petry's butcher shop have a slaughterhouse attached to his business?' asked Campbell.

'Yes,' she replied.

'Could your son have seen the process?' asked Campbell.

Suspicion started to appear around the corners of the woman's tired eyes, but she answered, 'Yes, of course, Inspector. We come from a family of butchers. It gives us a balanced view of life. Death is part of the natural cycle.'

'How many sons do you have?' asked WPC Jenner.

Sarah Twilling turned to look at the policewoman. From her face it was obvious she'd forgotten that the officer was there. 'Just the one.' She turned back to Campbell. Underneath her blotchy skin her face turned white. 'Why are you asking these questions, Inspector? Ernest could not have had anything to do with my husband's murder.'

Campbell looked into her eyes and muttered a curious, 'Oh?'

'He wouldn't do a thing like that. I know he wouldn't. And he didn't even know Kelvin Silverton.' Her eyes fluttered down. 'It was on the lunch time news. Karen had it on.' She looked at her screwed up hands.

'We have to look in all the nooks and crannies, Mrs Twilling. We also have to check out where people were at the time of Mr Silverton's death. It is a matter of routine.'

Campbell seemed to have soothed her enough to answer the question. She sounded lost as she said, 'I was here with Karen. We slept in the same room. This house is so big. I couldn't sleep on my own. I was scared of what I might dream.'

'Mrs Twilling.' Campbell said this firmly to gain her attention. 'Do you have any doctors in the family, or any friends that are doctors, or anyone who works at the hospital?'

'There are nearly two thousand people working at that hospital. Everyone around here knows someone who works there. But I know no-one well. I've not been allowed friends, Inspector.' What little was left of Sarah Twilling's composure was crumbling before them.

'Thank you, Mrs Twilling.' Campbell paused as he went to leave the room. 'Bye the way, I saw the funeral director leaving your step-son's cottage. We will let you know when the burial can go ahead.'

'I don't think you could have, Inspector. The funeral director came to me this morning. I am making the arrangements. They are nothing to do with him.' Through her exhaustion Campbell detected a flare of anger from Sarah Twilling at his remark.

'Apologies; that was an assumption on my part. Thank you again, Mrs Twilling,' said Campbell backing out of the room. He nodded 'Goodbye' to Karen Henderson and WPC Jenner did the same.

'Isn't Waverley's where the Middleton's son works?' asked Jenner. Campbell got in the car before agreeing with a Celtic grunt.

*      *      *

It was already five o'clock when Campbell and Jenner reached the gatehouse. The room lights were out and a light in the hall shone through an open door into the living room. Jonathan Twilling was not at home. Lifting the radio, Campbell arranged to have the owner traced through the number of the dark blue car and directed Jenner to drive back towards Ouse Crossing.

Campbell liked the town. The High Street and the river ran through the centre of it. The river ran east to west and the High Street, north to south. Where they met were two bridges. One was an eighteenth century stone arch, which now only took pedestrians, and the other was built after the second World War to take motorised traffic. Here the river was just wide and deep enough to take narrow boats because two smaller rivers joined just before they reached the town centre. Even in the town the river banks were shaded by large spreading trees. The late afternoon sun fired the autumn colours and the river water, giving the town a warm glow. The square Norman tower of the local church was placed on high ground to the east behind the shops. These buildings along the High Street were a mixture of old and new, being made mostly of red brick or finished in mock Tudor. The roofs were red, black or mottled colours. The windows were neatly and recently painted in white.

Waverley's was one of three butcher's shops in the High Street. Jenner drew up outside. A dark haired man with a pole had just finished putting away a brightly coloured awning. He stopped and leaned on his pole. 'Af'noon,' he said pleasantly. His green eyes twinkled at Jenner as she got out of the car. Campbell assessed his age at under twenty, and guessed that the eyes had been inherited from Sarah Twilling.

He interrupted the young man's wink at Jenner by saying, 'I'm looking for Ernest Petry. Police.' Campbell showed his identity card by way of explanation. The young man nodded and said that he was Ernest Petry, so Campbell continued, 'Your step-father was murdered a couple of days ago and last night one of his associates was murdered, Mr Kelvin Silverton.'

'I know that. It was on the news on the telly.'

'Your mother is very distressed,' said Jenner. Ernest smiled at her. Campbell saw that he was going to respond to her so he moved back a pace.

'I know. You think I should be with her holding her hand. She's so weak. She should have said "No" to Frederick Blasted Twilling. She makes me angry.' The smile had gone from his face. Ernest Petry was leaner than the Middleton's son and not as tall. His high cheek bones and sharp brow seemed to hide his eyes when they were not laughing.

'Because you love her,' said Jenner.

'I wouldn't kill for her, if that's what you mean? And there's no sibling rivalry either. Jonathan isn't my real brother,' said Ernest Petry. Campbell noticed how the Norfolk overtones in his voice slipped away as the young man's emotions rose.

Jenner continued, 'I never suggested there was. But you've thought about death, about killing?'

'Hasn't everybody played murder and suicide games in their heads? If I jump under this bus I'll die. If I push that person in front of that train I'll be a murderer.' Ernest stopped, wiped his soiled sleeve across his forehead, 'I hated my step-father and I'm not keen on his son either, but I didn't murder Frederick Twilling or Silverton.'

'No sibling rivalry then,' said Jenner sarcastically.

Ernest inspected his pole. 'In my opinion, it takes a certain sort of person to murder the Twillings and Silvertons of this world - someone who wants to get rid of all the rotten meat. It would almost be a religion with them. Such a person needs to kill and kill again.'

'We are not searching for your opinions, Mr Petry. Unless, of course, they represent inside knowledge of the murderer's motives?' Campbell raised himself onto the balls of his feet.

Ernest glanced at him and then back at Jenner. 'I've got alibis for the nights Fred Twilling and Kelvin Silverton were murdered. It's Jonathan Twilling you want to look at. He hates my mother. He's worried that his father might have left her enough to live on.' He seemed to have finished speaking until Mark Middleton came outside. Then Ernest added, looking at Campbell, 'Frederick Twilling was a bastard to everybody, Inspector. You only have to ask Mark here.'

The burly young man from the forest cottage nodded a greeting but his smooth brow was slightly folded in a frown.

'Tell the Inspector how Twilling stitched up your parents,' said Ernest Petry.

'It won't look good for my family, Ernie,' complained Mark.

'You and I are in the clear anyway. We were at that do in town with old Mr Waverley and the lot from the abattoir. We were there until late and then the old man took us home for drinks,' explained Ernest Petry. 'We couldn't have done Twilling in.'

Mark Middleton's frown remained, but Campbell could see he had decided that he was no longer in a position to keep these things to himself. 'My Mum and Dad were left some land on the outskirts of town, Ouse Crossing here. It was a small holding of about ten acres that my grandfather had worked. My parents saw it as a burden, but I told them with the town expanding the way it was it would be a good idea to apply for planning permission to build houses on it; then they could sell it for a lot of money. They applied but it was turned down. The planning office told them they were unlikely to ever get planning permission for that site. They called it a green-fields site, or something.' Mark paused and looked for encouragement from his audience.

Campbell managed an 'And?'

'My parents said, "I told you so," to me and were cross at the expense the application had caused them. There was the fee for the application, fees for the plans to be drawn up and solicitors' fees. They had to sell the land to pay their bills. Frederick Twilling stepped in and offered my parents a silly price, and they took it. Now Twilling has put in plans for an industrial estate on that same land.'

'Did he get permission to build?' asked Campbell.

'It was still going through at the Ouseland Council when he died. But he always got permission for whatever he wanted. That land is worth a fortune with planning consent,' grumbled Mark.

'What did your parents' solicitor advise?' asked Campbell.

'Nothing. My parents wouldn't go back to him,' said Mark. 'They were probably right. All these local solicitors are strung together like a well tied joint of meat. Kelvin Silverton, Twilling's solicitor, knew them all. They wouldn't do anything to upset one of their chums.' Mark stopped.

The man looked trapped, now was the time for Campbell to ask, 'Where were you both last night?'

'We share a flat together above the shop,' said Ernest Petry. 'Mr Waverley likes the security. We were there all night listening to music. We had a couple of girl friends over.'

'We'll have to check with them.' Campbell took the names of the women the young butchers claimed could vouch for their movements. His stomach told him it was time to make for home, so he turned away from them after thanking them for their co-operation and sat in the passenger seat of the car. When Jenner got in, he asked her if she would like to have some tea at his house as she would be keeping an eye on the Campbell children in the evening. She agreed, if Margaret wouldn't mind. Campbell assured her she would be most welcome and turned to his pocket notebook while Jenner drove.

He made a note to arrange for the other small butcher shops to be checked for the movements of their workers on the vital nights. He considered his jottings. All was unsettled in his world and his gut gnawed at him. He imagined tearing up that brochure of Margaret's, Campbell's Castle, and watching the pieces fall: fall like dead men never to be put together. Another night was coming. He felt a pang of desperation cut through him.

# Chapter 10

Catherine thought the girls seemed settled at Sadie's now after a night's sleep. Laura and Molly had found Sadie's toddlers in the kitchen and were playing with them. Catherine smiled as she watched. The twin boys were eighteen months or so old and they moved and expressed themselves in a way that reminded her of her own two children at that age. Unexpectedly, she found herself wishing that her two children were still tiny. Only because, she told herself, if they were between one and three they would be totally unaware of the happenings of the last few days. She wished she could forget everything too and let it all drift away as her worries had used to when Robert had wrapped her in his arms. She wasn't sure anymore if that had been a reality or a fantasy. It seemed so long ago, but she wanted it to be a reality. And she wanted it back.

Sitting on the third step from the bottom of the staircase she watched the sturdy wooden front door. The house was similar to her own in basic structure, but twice the size. The comfortable late Victorian houses with a front room on either side of the front door produced an image of Victorian sense and respectability that seemed out of keeping with her present circumstances. Catherine moved her fingers over the thick carpet. It was much thicker than her own, she noted. The furniture was finer here, the wood a better quality. The numerous ornaments recognised the foreign countries visited by at least one member of the family.

Sadie Groom came through the hall from the living room and asked Catherine if she was alright. She moved her head to lie that she was, and then, as Sadie walked on towards the kitchen, Catherine reached through the banister rails and caught her friend's arm.

'I saw Kelvin coming here the night before last,' she blurted out.

Catherine pulled in her lips as if trying to bring back the words that had spilled out of them.

'He came here looking for you,' said Sadie. 'He'd heard you were in trouble. Look, he was your solicitor. He wanted to help. I told him you'd just left and if he drove straight round to your house he would get there before you.'

'Why didn't you tell me?' said Catherine letting her grip loosen on her friend's arm.

'I didn't want to upset you. I didn't know you'd seen Kelvin call. But I did tell that policewoman who brought you round here yesterday that I'd seen him,' explained Sadie.

'I'm sorry. I thought... It doesn't matter.' Catherine's momentary anger had gone and left her tired. 'The police ask such questions. I even start to doubt my own innocence, let alone Robert's. Now he's missing, it's even worse. The police seem to think it confirms his guilt. They even cooked up a possible scheme between him and you. My mind is so muddled.'

'Look, go upstairs and get some rest. I'll see to this lot,' said Sadie gesturing in the direction of the children. Catherine couldn't cope with her friend's smile of motherly concern which she gave her as well as the children. Was it meant to be overwhelming? She held back her tears. They would crack what little emotional strength she had left, and she no longer wanted to show her weakness in front of Sadie.

The moment was broken by one of the twins screeching from the kitchen and Sadie left to attend to the child while Catherine climbed the stairs. The guest room smelled sweet and had chintz curtains over the front bay window and a matching bedspread, but the effect of this co-ordination was made excessive to Catherine by wallpaper with an identical but smaller flower print. Lying on the bed, she closed her eyes.

Her brain would not rest though. It analysed and pushed at memories. Where was Robert? If only she could have him back. Her wanting of him had become a craving, screaming, weeping noise inside her heart. It was like the sound of an up rush of hot air taking burning chaff up into the sky. Mingled with this was the smell of death, which she could not rid her nostrils of. 'God, I must think of other things,' she muttered.

She must've slept briefly for her next conscious thought rippled through her mind waking her. Sadie's reactions didn't feel right. Catherine had to make herself strong. 'Analyse,' she told herself.

Sadie seemed undisturbed by Robert's disappearance. Therefore, either she didn't care what had happened to him, or she knew where he was. Dear God, could the police have been right about her? Could Sadie and Robert have killed Kelvin Silverton? Catherine wondered what Sadie was really like under that long auburn hair and tall, slender frame. Why could beautiful people always appear good even though they were not? There was something dishonest in having blue eyes with auburn hair; shouldn't they be green or hazel? Catherine shook her head. She was back in the muddled gloom she thought she'd escaped.

But where was Sadie's husband? Catherine couldn't remember ever having seen him. Sadie had always maintained that she saw so little of him that when he was home they went to see his family or went on holiday for a month at a time. It seemed logical enough.

Catherine rolled off the bed and started to unpack the cases she'd left from the day before. She placed her girls' clothes in the drawers with her own. She opened the wardrobe. A few of Sadie's clothes were on one side of the wardrobe. All of these were designer labels and made with luxuriously soft fabric which swished smoothly when moved. There were stretchy figure hugging tubes and soft sheer silks that would drape over and flatter Sadie's long curves.

She did not feel envious, Catherine told herself, just impressed. Then she felt the absence of Robert: his clothes: his heavy jackets; male shaped trousers. She smiled and wept at the banality of caring about clothes.

The street outside was never very busy so she heard clearly the click of a car door carried on the morning air up to her open window. She moved towards the sound and pulled the edge of the curtain away from the wall. The rest of the curtain remained still. She knew she could not be seen from this position.

A man came out of the driver's seat of a dark blue car. Catherine couldn't see from her elevated position whether there was anyone else in it. He came through the iron-gate and up the garden path. His right hand reached up to the door-bell. She could not see his face fully, only his forehead and the end of his nose and grey hair above his ears. She could not see Sadie standing in the doorway either. All she could hear were their muffled voices. They were talking in an unnaturally hushed way, even so wisps of the conversation reached up to Catherine's window, such as, 'She's staying with me,' from Sadie. The male voice was deeper and quieter. It might have been because the sound was being blocked by his head, but she was sure he said, 'Lucky'. They talked some more, but no matter how she strained she could hear nothing more of their conversation. She wanted to know why they were talking about her, but she was too afraid to call out, for herself and because Molly and Laura were in the house.

As the man started to turn away from Sadie, a bird flew into Catherine's window, not seeing the glass. The man looked up at the thud it made.

Catherine jumped, but did not fail to note the man's features. His face was a series of balls; even his forehead seemed to have a circular shape in its centre. His nose was short and bulbous and his chin made a matching set of facial balls. His cheeks had lost some of their roundness and firmness over the years. This seemed to clash with his physique, which had seemed strong but lean when she'd seen him walk from the gate. His top lip was in the shape of a long-bow with the centre line stretched like a bow-string into a permanent smile. It had the same level of honesty as a door to door salesman, thought Catherine.

It wasn't until the man started to walk away on his soft brown shoes that she recognised him. His grey hair was cropped at his green and white striped collar, but above his grey hair the top of his head was naked. A smooth burnished circle of skin glowed in the late morning sun. The only place that did not shine was a circular area the size of a coin. The position of the mole was unmistakable. It was the distinguishing mark of the third man she'd seen in the car park with Fred Twilling and Mercer.

Her first reaction was to want to follow this man, but she knew she couldn't leave her daughters. The second one was to alert the police about him, but she could not do that here in Sadie's own house. If this man was involved with Frederick Twilling, Sadie could be entangled with them also.

Perhaps, she and the girls were in danger, wondered Catherine. She didn't know. But, surely, Sadie wouldn't allow anything to happen in her house while her own boys were around? If there was any possible risk to Catherine's children, she would have to do something about it.

Catherine started refilling one of the suitcases with her children's clothes. The dreaded visit to Evelyn seemed like an escape. She spotted the bottle of perfume on the side table and realised that was why she felt odd. This was the cause of the sweet smell she'd barely noticed when she'd first come into the room. She wriggled the glass stopper. It was loose so she tightened it and went to the window for air. Feeling better she left the suitcase and started down the stairs to tell Molly and Laura that they would be staying with their grandmother. But the pile on the stair carpet folded under her foot and Catherine slipped on the step she'd been sitting on that morning. Its traditional paisley pattern danced before her eyes. Sadie came out of the front room. She was saying something. It could have been, 'Are you alright?' but all Catherine could see was her mouth moving. Suddenly Sadie's face seemed to be too close and then it seemed too far away.

'Where's Robert? Please, Sadie, where is he?' Catherine grasped at her friend. She wanted her face to stand still. She wanted some truth, some reality. She caught a handful of auburn hair.

'Look you've had a shock. You'll be alright. We'll take you upstairs to lie down,' Sadie said.

"Is that all she can say," thought Catherine.

Laura appeared in the doorway. Her shoulder length golden hair framed her pale face and her anxious brown eyes. Catherine hurt at the sight of them, how they looked like her husband's. But they were different to his. The strength her daughter had found two days ago was still there. Catherine felt the courage flow over her as Laura wrapped her slender arms about her and held her tight. The girl was whispering in her ear, warm, reassuring, childish things. She called her, 'Mummy'. Then the words started to form phrases which showed that they came from a growing and understanding child. They tapped some deep well of resolve and strength inside Catherine. She held her daughter tightly allowing only a few tears to spill out of her eyes. Then she held the girl's shoulders and moved her to arms' length.

'Thank you. I'll be fine now,' said Catherine. Her vision had returned to normal, and her body seemed unharmed. The effect of the perfume was wearing off. She could no longer quiz Sadie, though, with the children watching. 'I think I'd better take you two over to Evelyn's.' Molly and Laura started to moan so she carried on quickly, 'Yes, I've made up my mind. I know she's cranky, but she's your grandmother.' The word 'grandmother' seemed wholly inappropriate, but to convince herself that Evelyn must have some love in her somewhere, she used it again. 'Your grandmother will take care of you, and you'll be out of the way of the press. It won't be long before they track me down here, and if I stay here they won't go around Evelyn's looking.' It sounded a lame excuse, but they seemed to accept it.

She wanted to come back by herself and talk to Sadie. She could be wrong about her suspicions. It didn't seem fare to tell the police before speaking to her friend. What could she tell them anyway: Sadie Groom knows a man, who knows Mercer and knew the deceased Frederick Twilling? It sounded like telling tales to her, like pointing the finger at someone else because she felt guilty herself. She kept feeling guilty and yet she knew she hadn't done anything wrong. All those years of her mother blaming her for everything was the cause, she was sure. And, of course, there was Kelvin.

The children's suitcase was taken down to the bottom of the back garden to Sadie's timber garage. The double doors opened onto a lane which ran down between two sets of rear gardens with allotments at the end. There were garages lining it on both sides. Although her head was now quite clear Catherine asked Sadie to drive it out of the garage -- she didn't trust herself to do this with a borrowed car. They loaded it with the children and the luggage and Catherine laid her coat on the seat between the children. When the car, a BMW, stood glinting in the sun, Catherine slid into the driver's seat that Sadie had just left. It was soothing to be enveloped by luxury.

She mouthed, 'Bye', to Sadie and sighed with relief. As the car turned towards Evelyn's she began to wonder if the open perfume bottle in her room had been done on purpose. So she tried to strike up a conversation with her daughters, hoping the sound of their voices would chase away her fears. 'George will be there. You like George,' she said. But the girls were silent so her thoughts came to her like demons.

She wanted to blank out any conscious thinking of the horrors she had seen, but they were fighting for attention, making her put a pattern to these events, trying to make her seek some direction for the illogical happenings. She couldn't believe what the police had said about her being a victim. She was sure all that had happened was because of Frederick Twilling and his sharp practices. Someone knew where Robert was. Perhaps this man with the mole on his head would be able to tell everyone the truth. But she feared the truth. She wanted to know it and she didn't want to know it. What if the truth was that her husband had murdered these people? Had he run away out of fear, as she believed, or out of guilt? Had he been taken because he knew things he wasn't supposed to about the Twilling Empire? She didn't emotionally or logically know. She just wanted Robert back and if he was the murderer she wished he had murdered her there in the woods.

Her dark blonde hair, despite being short, flicked into her face as she shook her head. The movement jolted the steering wheel and she clipped the verge of the road. 'I'm sorry girls. I wasn't concentrating,' Catherine said. With a glance in her mirror she noticed Laura's face. It was worried. She could see Molly too, but she just looked mildly surprised. 'I'm alright, honestly,' she said for Laura's benefit. She wanted to mean it.

Now she concentrated on the road. Ordinarily she would have barely grasped certain key landmarks that marked their progress, but she was aware that her nervous state had pushed her surroundings into sharp focus. There was the flint cottage where the unscathed faces had allowed her and Robert, at gun point, to phone the police. Then there was the even woodland planted in neat rows with, Catherine thought, the formality of an unnatural mind. The straight trunks, bred for their destiny as telegraph poles or chipboard, swayed in the breeze.

The day had turned grey and the shadows among the trees prevented the casual onlooker from penetrating its depths. She remembered clearly the place she'd stopped that night. She saw the crushed vegetation on the verge with a line of ferns beginning to brown between this and the trees. There were over ripe briers making their criss-cross patterns like giant cobwebs between the trunks. It had been so quiet that night: only the sound of Robert behind her. Had she heard a car moving away? She'd told the police, 'No'. But had she? She'd heard no screams from Frederick Twilling or from Kelvin Silverton. They had received such silent deaths, and they had not been the sort of men to accept their gruesome fate without a savage cling to life.

'Do we have to stay at Evelyn's? She's so cranky?' complained Molly.

'She's just old,' lied Catherine. Her mother was not even fifty.

'Look out, Mum,' Laura and Molly screamed as a red car pulled out of one of the woodland tracks and shot across their path. Catherine jammed on the brakes and turned the steering wheel so the BMW veered onto the grass verge.

In a moment Catherine had seen the occupant of the car. She'd noticed his ginger hair and beard. His face was so brightly coloured with temper that it clashed with his facial trimmings. For such minor mishaps the defence mechanism of an amusing thought lightened the load. He gave her a stare that told her she was a stupid woman who hadn't the sense to stop when he cared to join the main road from a blind lane between trees. Catherine mouthed some abuse through the windscreen in return. Then she turned to the girls, 'I should have seen him,' she said.

'It was his fault, Mum,' said Laura. 'Not yours.'

'Yes. Yes it was,' agreed Catherine.

At the start of Hillvill she remembered the town of her youth with its river running along the bottom of the hill to the west of the town. Most of the buildings had been built on the hill to avoid flooding so there were only a few poor cottages by the river. Even the more recent buildings were built near the eastern by-pass despite the reduction of flood risk due to the building of cuts, dykes and sluices to control the water.

In the town itself, which Catherine avoided if she could, the yellow bricked buildings were greyed by grime and their black slate roofs were made uneven by poor repair. The buildings were mostly two storeys with the odd three storey construction between. A hundred years before these would have been important busy places, but many of them were empty with bare and broken upper windows. On the ground floor of the buildings shops fitted with modern windows and displaying modern goods denied the decay above them while the wealthy business people lived on the outskirts of town.

With relief Catherine turned her borrowed car past the 'For Sale' sign, which poked out from the hedge of Evelyn's next door neighbour, and into her mother's drive.

The windows to her childhood home were shut, and the garage was shut too. Catherine walked around to the back of the house leaving Molly and Laura in the car. A cold wind came off the fens and cut around her, flaying her hair into jagged shapes. Beyond the river at the bottom of the hill, fields of mottled gold stretched to the lines of mist between the land and the sky. These were fields of straw stubble. She turned towards the greenhouses and sheds. She called, 'Evelyn' and 'George' in vain. Evelyn's house was the last one on Tonne Road so the house for sale was the only neighbour. Catherine peered over into its garden, but it was obviously empty with its curtain-less windows and grass pushing through the cracked concrete that surrounded one of its large square sheds.

As she walked back towards the house she heard her mother's car pull into the driveway. She saw Evelyn park it next to the BMW and beckon to her.

'You said your car was broken down,' Catherine accused her as Evelyn stretched her legs out of the car.

'It was. Without Robert around to fix it I took it to the garage.'

'You could do that every time,' Catherine muttered, but she knew Evelyn heard.

'Why should I?' she retorted. 'Robert's perfectly capable of maintaining our cars. That's why George and I had the same as yours.' Catherine looked at her mother's car. The one in front of her was identical to her own. It was a middle sized car with a hatch back. The only difference was the colour, her mother's was a mid-blue and hers and Robert's was light blue. George's was white.

Suddenly the silvery BMW seemed alien to Catherine. The door seemed unduly solid as she opened it for Laura and Molly to slide out.

'We've had the odd neighbour snooping,' said Catherine. 'Even though I'm at Sadie's I think the press will soon find me. I wonder if you could have the girls for a few days?'

'I'm a doctor, not a nanny,' said Evelyn.

'You wanted us to come over,' said Catherine. 'I thought you were having some extended leave?'

'George told you, I suppose,' said Evelyn.

'Yes,' said Catherine.

'Blast George,' said Evelyn. 'Where is he anyway?'

'I don't know. I couldn't find him.'

'He's been a blasted nuisance since that dog died,' said Evelyn. Her grey eyes flicked from side to side as if searching the garden.

Catherine thought how youthful she still looked, but even this could not make her like her.

Her mother's gaze settled back on her daughter. 'So you want me to look after your off-spring, do you?' Evelyn smiled. Catherine didn't want to analyse it, but she found she was doing so out of habit. There was definitely triumph in the corners of Evelyn's mouth. It was rapidly softened when Catherine looked at it, but she had seen it before it was disguised.

'You trust me, don't you?' demanded Evelyn.

'Yes,' replied Catherine, resolving to pick up the children as soon as possible. Her mother would make her pay a thousand times for this small favour. Evelyn went to say something but Catherine cut her off by saying, 'I can't stop.' Her mother's demands would have to wait.

Stepping back into the BMW she was grateful for that physical distance which opened up between herself and Evelyn. But, when she shut the door, she was suddenly alone. Her family was gone. The silence was not soothing, it was oppressive. She smiled and waved at the girls and her mother, wishing that Evelyn could be like other mothers and grandmothers. She turned the ignition key and the engine purred into life.

The wheels rolled the BMW backwards, and Catherine was on the road again. She checked herself. Her hands were steady and so was her head. At the traffic lights she pointed the car eastwards, towards higher ground, away from the black fen and towards Ouse Crossing. She knew her children were now safe. Even though Evelyn didn't like it, at least Molly and Laura were away from Sadie's house. She could now talk to Sadie, learn what she knew about Robert; perhaps even find him.

The relief poured itself into a long sigh until a shiver started beneath the skin of her shoulders and worked its way down her back to be absorbed by the seat of the car. She allowed herself to drive automatically, her mind pleasantly empty. So much could have been thought about. This time it was simple to think of nothing and become absorbed by the piano concerto that twirled and fiddled in her ears from Sadie's music collection.

Her fingers moved the rear view mirror. In it she checked behind her. There was a red car. It was a Ford similar to her own, common enough, but she recognised the number plate. It had to be the same vehicle: the red car. The one she'd had to brake for on her journey to Evelyn's. The BMW passed into the shade of the forest. The red Ford followed. Its windscreen reflected the angled patterns of the trees. The flickering shapes obscured anything beyond its mirror. Was it the same driver, she wondered.

# Chapter 11

Swearing softly Catherine grasped the steering wheel of Sadie's BMW so that her palms stung. Then she curled her fingers around it stabbing the heels of her hands with her finger nails as she pushed her weight through her leg and foot onto the accelerator.

She smiled. She felt thrilled by the sudden movement. She felt powerful, revenged; free. The BMW was fast. She could accelerate and be away. She glanced back in the mirror. The car behind had not accelerated as fast but it was gradually reaching her. The vehicle behind her must have a more powerful engine than her own car, she decided, because it would not have been able to accelerate like that. Her euphoria left her. The BMW could, no doubt, go faster, but she knew she was not capable of driving at higher speeds than this. She would crash. She would be safely dead. But her daughters would be motherless.

Catherine watched the red car come up close behind her. It pulled out sharply, rolling on its suspension. It rode level with her using the lane for on-coming traffic. She tried to keep her face firmly to the front, but she couldn't stop herself looking at the driver.

She remembered the face with its red hair and red skin. It was the same driver that had shot out in front of her earlier, though his eyes were now hidden by sunglasses. She could still feel the look of hate through them. Looking at him made her doubt her own sanity as well as his. She wracked her brain. She didn't know him... from anywhere. Still the red car was next to her. The speed they were travelling at was frightening. And, why was he here? He could just be a crank who had taken an immediate and intense dislike to her, or he could be here because of the deaths of Frederick Twilling and Kelvin Silverton. Her memory of him started at the moment he had pulled out on her from one of the forest lanes.

Whoever he was, he was here, next to her, driving on the wrong side of the road. It had been straight and empty for some distance, but now it started to curve away. Catherine pressed the brake pedal as hard and fast as she could. The front of the BMW dipped from the sudden change of pace. She was pushed forward as it slowed. She braced herself against the steering wheel and the seat belt bit into her shoulder. She saw the driver of the red car turn to see where she had gone and, at that moment, a lorry appeared out of the shadows on the same side of the road as the red car and it was heading towards it.

Catherine was now stationary. There'd been no vehicles behind her so it had been safe to stop. She crouched over her steering wheel covering her head with her arms to protect herself from the crash of the lorry with the red car but there was no sound of rubber losing its grip on the tarmac or of splintering metal. Instead the lorry went by her sounding its collection of differently pitched horns loudly. She opened her eyes to see the red car in the same lane as herself reversing towards her at high speed.

Cold beads of water escaped from her skin and dampened her dress. The engine was still running, but the BMW was not moving. She stared at his black sunglasses framed by the rear windscreen of the red car. She feared for her life. Catherine rummaged with the gears; her co-ordination was lost to her. She was focussing on something he was holding up in his hand so she could see it. It was a photograph, a portrait. She couldn't see the picture clearly but recognised the grey card mounting as the sort used by school photographers. She knew that because she had such a picture at home, in her living room -- the one taken last term of her daughters. Oh God, Laura, Molly, please keep them safe.

Having the picture was sure to mean he'd broken into her home to take it. This was a threat to her, to her daughters. Her every nerve was honed to protect them. She had to stay and see what this man wanted, so she locked the doors against him and watched him walk the short distance between the two vehicles in long powerful strides. He held the photograph up to the passenger side window. The faces of Molly and Laura smiled from the paper through the glass and into Catherine like sharp knives thrust into her lungs.

'Did you think your girlies were safe with your mum, Mrs Fenman?' asked the red haired man. His voice was a series of grunts shaped into the local accent. 'I saw you take them,' he said. 'Do you think they're still there?

I was sent to get you. Open the door and we'll not hurt them.'

Catherine lifted her hands to hit him with both fists as he got in, but he smiled at her, goading her. She knew he would enjoy hitting her back.

'Think of your kids,' he said, 'and do as I say.' She told herself to suppress her anger and panic, which seemed to be fighting each other for control over her. She knew she would have to do as she was told by this man. He was threatening her with her children's safety.

He told her to drive. She went to ask him who he was, but he growled, 'I don't want no questions,' so she bit hard into her upper lip.

The car moved forwards while her mind sought an answer to this man's actions. He was certainly likely to hurt her which confirmed her fear for her children. But could that mean he was the murderer of Frederick Twilling and Kelvin Silverton? Could he have taken or killed… She didn't want to use her husband's name in that sentence.

The red haired man told her to turn left. She did so. They were moving south. Catherine felt the closeness of the high, trimmed hedges rather than saw them. She vaguely recognised the road: but it was not one she used often. It felt as if someone had turned on a remote control switch somewhere inside her brain. The man told her to turn left again.

'Are they here?' she asked.

'You've just left them at your mother's house,' snarled the man. 'They aren't here.'

Catherine blinked, her blood chilled.

A narrow opening with a neat blue gate appeared from among the hedgerow nearest them. The gate stood open, beyond lay a track. The large car wouldn't go through, Catherine was sure. After three attempts she drove up onto the grass verge. She was shaking from trying to control her anger which had all but destroyed her fear and panic.

'I can't do it,' she said. Her voice was stronger than she'd expected. 'You'll have to drive it, if you want it through there.'

'Don't you understand, woman? I got a mate over there with them at your posh old mother's house.'

She yanked at his clothes as if she could pull her children from him. He replied with a sharp slap across her face.

He pushed her out of the car and leapt out after her. Then he started to shove her along the track. She tried to keep her sense of direction ready for any escape she could make. The gate would have been wide enough for the car, Catherine decided, if she hadn't been so shaken. Tractors must have come down this way frequently as the ground had been made firm by layers of pressed gravel. She thought her captor dragged her west for about a quarter of a mile until the track turned south. It disappeared into a spinney so she could only guess that it would join back onto the main road.

Beyond the bend a concrete apron spread over a large area. It was empty except for a pile of broken timber pallets. Beyond the concrete stood a building with a curved metal roof which formed a black semicircle against the clouds. Catherine recognised the type of building; they were common in this area. They were left over military buildings from the Second World War. The farmers had used them since to store equipment and crops. This one stood with its doors open. Catherine smelt the air as she approached. It was dank with the odour of rotten potatoes. She looked in the Nissan hut; it was dark towards the back: she couldn't see any soil covered vegetables. Perhaps, it was being aired ready for this year's crop. She stopped in front of the building.

The red haired man pushed her through the door. She knew his motive was not a sexual one. Somehow she'd never thought it was. The walk had helped to clear her mind.

'There is no one holding my mother and children, is there?' she asked.

His sneer told her she had been tricked into coming here by the threat against her children. Catherine leapt on him. Her fist caught his jaw before he could protect it, but he pushed her away easily, his height and strength far exceeded hers. His arm went back to strike a heavy blow and stopped. She stood and looked at him with complete loathing. She no longer cared for her own safety and, freed from the fear of harm coming to her children, she demanded, 'Tell me why you have gone to all this trouble to get me here?'

'You are a criminal, Mrs Fenman,' replied a different voice from that of the red haired man. The voice came from inside the store. It had come from the depths of the building and rattled around its metallic side walls. Its pure tones were quite unlike the heavy local accent of the red haired man.

Catherine recognised the owner of the voice as he moved towards her. She'd seen him at the Council offices and his picture was regularly in the local paper. He was the son of Frederick Twilling, Jonathan. His pale complexion looked ghastly in the gloom. The protective anger she'd felt for her children was replaced by a fury at the way he'd chosen to meet her. He had tried to frighten her and he had succeeded.

While she was still stunned at finding herself brought before this man in this way, the red haired man, flushed with temper and exertion, pushed her down onto a pile of pallets just inside the door.

'Thank you, Nick,' said Jonathan to the red haired man. 'I can take it from here.' Nick stood aside.

The pallets dug into her back when she fell onto them and before she could sit up straight Jonathan Twilling had lowered himself into a position with his face over hers and just the thickness of a hand distance between them. Catherine could see that Jonathan Twilling enjoyed this chance to intimidate a person without risk to himself. He was too close. She didn't want to breathe in air that had been in his lungs so she tried to move her face away, but he stopped her by gripping her jaw.

He let go of it with a little painful twist and then he yelled at her, 'Why did you and that cowardly shit of a husband of yours kill my father? And Kelvin?' He shouted this question again and again between abusive phrases and knocking Catherine's shoulders to keep her off balance and unable to lash out at him. He did not seem to want the answers at first because he would not let her speak. So when the emotion started to drain from him and he stopped yelling, she decided not to answer him.

Even if this was not the behaviour of a man who had killed his father and his best friend, why should she tell him anything – not that she knew anything – when he treated her this way. And she couldn't say anything that would clear Robert's name, except her faith in him and that was not as rock solid as it should be. It was safest to deprive Jonathan of her co-operation. She stared at him until he shook his head and said,

'I want you to confess.'

'I haven't done anything,' said Catherine, quietly but firmly. Jonathan Twilling moved away. She leaned back for a moment, exhausted, her legs dangling over the edge of the pallets. Then she pushed herself up and watched his waxen figure move about the building. One minute he would be stiff with un-flexing limbs, the next moment he would be thrashing the tin walls with his fists, turning the metal and brick building into a furious and unrelenting drum.

Catherine stood up. She screamed a loud, full scream. It was meant as an act of war. Nick was back next to her. He tried to cover her mouth with his hand, but he was slow and fumbling so she bit him and continued to scream. She was hitting him too until she felt her arms pinned to her sides. She saw Jonathan Twilling coming towards her, a piece of wood from one of the broken pallets raised above his head.

He was going to beat her to death, she was sure. 'I didn't kill your father. I don't know who killed your father. Or Kelvin Silverton. I wouldn't kill Kelvin.' Her words were an attack, not a plea.

'I knew you and Kelvin were lovers,' said Jonathan Twilling. He wasn't just my solicitor he was my closest friend. I knew everything about him.' He looked at her and said, 'People kill their lovers.' The wood was still threatening.

'Not because they've lost interest in them, as I had done,' said Catherine barring her teeth at him. 'And as you knew him so well you will know he had no feelings for me.' At that moment she hated him. She did feel murderous.

Jonathan Twilling swore at her. 'Your husband would have wanted to kill him,' he said.

'I doubt it. I doubt if he cared.' Catherine knew that was a lie. She knew he cared. But he hadn't fought for her either. He'd accepted it as a declaration of his inadequacies as a husband. The eventual purpose of the affair from Catherine's point of view had failed. Now all she wanted to do was remove those events from her life.

The loss of Robert was aching inside her. She wanted to call it grief, but she dared not because she feared her body was telling her he was already dead. "How dare he pain and worry me by his absence," she thought, "The same way I'd dared pain him with Kelvin Silverton?" Catherine couldn't stop the tears coming to her eyes no matter how hard she held onto her breath, a couple escaped from her tear ducts. She turned and started to leave.

The lump of wood was wavering in Jonathan's hand. 'Let her go,' called Jonathan Twilling to Nick, now waiting just outside the Nissan hut. Catherine saw Jonathan's anger leave him and fatigue take over. She wondered if she had convinced him of her innocence or whether it was just a mood swing. Was he only mad with grief, or was he insane? She couldn't tell. But, she could understand his mistake because she knew that her discovery of the murder of Frederick Twilling so soon after his slaughter and then her finding Kelvin Silverton's body on her own property made her look guilty. And, that scared her more than anything else.

She ran out of the building past Nick and into another man. This one put his arms around her in a protective way. The embrace felt unfamiliar, and she would not be trapped again so she pulled away using the remaining power of her temper.

She went to flee, but the man she'd run into, Donald Mercer, said to her, 'Please stay. It is important.' And Catherine saw from the face of her husband's superior that it was.

'I see you've got a thug working for you now. Is that the way the business is going now your father's dead?' asked Mercer. 'You've been stupid, Twilling,' he continued. The strange way he pulled at his 'i's and 'e's gave strength to his words. 'This isn't the way. Let the police find out what happened. If she is guilty, they will deal, with it. And if you are guilty, they will deal with you.'

The young man swore again and leapt towards Mercer. 'What do you mean?'

'You were always arguing with your father. You could have easily got carried away,' said Mercer. The pale man still held the piece of pallet. 'And what you and Silverton were up to is anybody's guess. It could be that you want to blame someone else to hide your own guilt?'

'Why shouldn't I accuse her? The police are looking for her husband, anyway,' said Jonathan Twilling, 'Everyone knows that.'

'That doesn't make him guilty either,' said Mercer.

'Perhaps you know something I don't. You could have killed my father,' said Jonathan Twilling moving forward again.

'No, of course I didn't,' said Mercer. Catherine thought he said this a little too casually. 'I am a witness to your activities this afternoon, Twilling, so calm down before you make things worse for yourself.' Jonathan Twilling moved back throwing the lump of pallet against the wall of the hut. Its hollow clatter came out to Catherine as she walked away in the thin bright sunlight. 'We're going now,' added Mercer.

Back at the BMW Mercer took the driving seat. Catherine looked round but could not see his car. She wondered if it had been parked beyond the spinney. It seemed strange that he should have come to the potato store when he did. She had been calmed by his control and his smooth voice but now, away from the threat of Jonathan Twilling, all her old dislikes for Mercer came crowding in on her. She knew his charm was a tool to him and he used it to get what he wanted. Robert had not trusted him either and he was missing.

She felt uneasy about becoming Mercer's passenger and trembled as she opened the passenger door.

# Chapter 12

Looking at the side of Mercer's face from the passenger doorway, Catherine asked, 'How did you arrive at the hut as I was leaving?' She wouldn't get into the car until he gave her a reasonable answer.

'I had a meeting with Jonathan earlier,' replied Mercer. 'He left in a hurry and I didn't trust him, so I followed him up there. I saw you arrive with that new red necked heavy of Jonathan's. He's certainly changing the business since his father's death. I wanted to know what they were up to, so I watched.'

The reply partly reassured her. He sounded interested in her safety. It was only the fact that he hadn't tried to rescue her from Jonathan Twilling earlier when he had been there before her arrival which prevented her being completely satisfied. A moment later she smiled, hadn't Robert once called Mercer a coward? Robert's boss had waited until she'd freed herself.

'What meeting with Jonathan Twilling?' she asked.

'Get in, Catherine. I need to talk to you.'

She got in. They were already travelling quickly when he asked her where Robert was. 'Do you think I know?' Catherine yelled at him. She wanted to explode. 'Dear God, would I be here being pestered by police, bullied by Twilling and quizzed by you, if I knew where he was? I would be there too.'

'It's alright, Catherine. I just had to check,' said Mercer without taking his eyes from the road.

She knew he felt in control of her and she resented that. Now she had to ask him a question to push him off balance as he had done to her. She had to make it sound as if she thought Mercer was guilty of a misdeed. 'Does that mean you don't know where Robert is?' she asked.

It didn't fluster him, 'I haven't a clue, Catherine,' he replied, 'or would I be asking you. You've had a fright. Calm Down.'

She wanted to call him a 'condescending pig', but stopped herself. 'What was your meeting with Jonathan Twilling about?' asked Catherine again. Mercer seemed as if he was about to answer when his attention was taken by a car overtaking in the opposite direction without enough room.

When the car had passed safely his reply didn't answer the question, 'He's nasty. You've seen that. I think he could easily have killed his father, Kelvin and Robert.'

He had put her silent fear into words, 'Robert', 'killed'. These words stabbed into her stomach. She didn't want her husband to be dead. How she had toyed with the idea in the past: how she would live, what she would do. What foolishness it had all been, she wanted him. She could not stand being deprived of him. She choked and heard Mercer apologise for upsetting her.

Catherine didn't want to talk so she looked out of the car window, watching the countryside change into town as they crossed the by-pass. The gaping sides of the large warehouses and factories seemed vulgar to her in their single coloured whiteness or blueness. Without trees to dress them they seemed rudely bare. Suddenly she knew Robert wasn't dead. She would know if he was, instinctively. Mercer drove Sadie's BMW under the rail bridge, turned right towards the town centre and went past the turnings to Sadie's and then Catherine's street.

'I want to go back to Sadie's,' said Catherine.

'I need to talk to you,' said Mercer.

'Sadie's expecting me back. I'm late already,' said Catherine looking at the clock in the car. It said four pm. 'I'm staying at Sadie's. She will be worried about me.' But she didn't feel convinced that Sadie would care. She was no longer sure Sadie's feelings were those of a friend.

A mile later Mercer stopped the car on a green open space. The river ribboned past unseen below its sticky black banks. Its water was depleted from the summer's sun and it was still waiting for the autumn rains. The trees were different here from the forest. With the moisture from the river broad trunks grew to support spreading branches. The weather had changed again. The afternoon sun had strengthened and managed to break through the grey clouds. An area of blue sky was above the trees. Their golden leaves seemed to have captured the rays as they passed through them, Catherine wanted that brightness. She got out of the car and she put out her hand and watched the light patterns change across it. She saw a bench standing on the grass a short distance away. Mercer joined her from the car and, holding her arm, steered her towards the seat.

'I have to explain,' he said.

Catherine looked at him. He was being charming again. What was it he wanted from her?

'I suspended Robert from his job,' said Mercer. 'I knew Frederick Twilling was lying about Robert hitting him. I knew it was just the two of them on that field. There were no witnesses. There was no case against him.'

Catherine lifted her arm and tried to pull it away from him. Did he think a confession would gain her forgiveness?

He caught her wrist. 'Wait let me explain. You must understand. I want to get out of all this. I don't know why I got involved.'

'You're a first class cheat and liar,' said Catherine angrily.

'I know,' said Mercer. 'I had to suspend your husband, he knew about me. I used the usual procedure for a complaint being made against a council officer.'

Catherine wanted to ask what he thought Robert knew about Mercer, but wondered what the consequence of that knowledge would be for her. Her husband had, after all, disappeared.

'If Robert hadn't been so moral, more apathetic – like the rest of us – he wouldn't have had anything to tell Reede.'

'Reede? Who's Reede?' asked Catherine.

'You've seen him,' said Mercer. 'The day Fred Twilling died you were in the car park while we were talking. There was Fred Twilling, Reede and myself. I saw you with Robert.'

'Is Reede the man with the mole on his head?' asked Catherine.

'Yes, I think he has a mole,' said Mercer tweaking his words, thoughtfully slowing them down. 'He was investigating Twilling's activities.'

'Fraud squad?' guessed Catherine.

'No, he was a private investigator,' said Mercer. 'I don't know who had hired him, but he would have had to hand his knowledge over to the police. There were things I couldn't tell Reede.' Mercer looked at her face for the first time.

Sadie was not some enemy because she knew Reede. Reede was after the truth. With relief Catherine realised the perfume in her bedroom had been an accident.

Catherine felt Mercer's pleading gaze upon her. It made her uncomfortable.

'You must not tell Reede what Robert has told you. I would have to resign my post. I would never get another job,' he said.

Robert had told her nothing. She did not know whether to pretend he had told her and place herself in the same situation he had been in before his disappearance or to tell the truth, but perhaps Mercer wouldn't believe that she knew nothing. He was certainly talking to her as if she knew all about him. Before she'd decided what to say on this matter a simple repulsion for Mercer took over. 'Why should I care about your work?' she asked.

'I'm not asking you to care. If you implicate me, I will implicate Robert,' said Mercer, still looking at her face.

She looked away. Catherine didn't know what was going on so she didn't know how Mercer could make Robert look guilty but the police must be gathering evidence against her and her husband for the murders. She could not risk Mercer telling them anything even if it were a lie. Mercer could lie so well. His suspension of Robert told her that.

The late afternoon sun started to thin and a cold breeze moved along the river bank. They were seated on a triangle of land between the joining of two rivers. The breeze seemed to come up from both of them chilling the air.

She nodded to show him she would keep her silence to protect her husband. Catherine wasn't sure she wanted to hear what he said if it were to endanger her. Yet her nod had obviously been taken as prior knowledge of Mercer's activities. Then Mercer started to talk with the need of someone who'd kept something to himself for a long time. His voice sounded urgent, yet all the things he spoke of were safely in the past.

'Mrs Twilling, Fred's wife, was formerly Mrs Petry. She's been a councillor on the planning committee for some time. She always stands up dutifully and declares her interests before a debate on an issue that would affect her financially. You know this procedure is there so that decisions can be made with everyone aware of the situation?'

'They have to declare their interests, I know that,' said Catherine.

He continued, 'And I know that she has agreements with other committee members.' Mercer distorted his voice to imitate a lady with a refined voice talking in a hushed whisper, 'If I want one of Fred's proposals to be accepted, you give it a "Yes" vote and I'll give you a "Yes" vote for something you want in your area that you've had to declare an interest in.'

He changed back to his normal precise speech. 'She has arrangements with many other councillors. These people don't really care what happens in other villages or towns. They only care about how fat they can make their wallets. That's why they stand for the council in the first place. Everything looks nice and democratic while the councillors get what they want. The sad thing is Mrs Petry was different before she met Fred Twilling. And he was manipulating her long before they were married.'

'Did you tell Reede?' she quizzed.

'Yes, I told him about the corruption among the councillors,' said Mercer. 'But if you give people like Reede a lead they will follow it. Anyway, you know as well as I do that these things go on everywhere?'

Catherine didn't but said nothing.

Mercer continued, 'It was the land deals that gave Fred Twilling the edge. It was remarkably simple. Fred arranged for planning officers to tell the owners of pockets of land he wanted that they would never get planning consent to build on them. The officers even went as far as to recommend to the committee that permission should not be given if these people actually got as far as putting in applications for buildings or whatever.'

'But you make the recommendations to the committee,' said Catherine. 'You were the one making those decisions.'

'This has been going on for years. The whole thing was well established even before I arrived here. And it was not just me, or Sarah Twilling. He had his first wife on the council. I think that's what made her ill. And, that's how he met up with Sarah. To work, Fred's "friendships" had to extend to other officers within the council.' Mercer was looking upwards. Catherine wondered if he was looking for forgiveness or inspiration. She would not give him either. After a moment he said, 'Then Fred Twilling would buy the land off them at a low price, he would apply for planning permission, and he would get it. Land is always worth more with permission for development. And Frederick Twilling could afford to hang onto land for years. He's owned fields where the town's superstores, petrol stations and gravel quarries are, as well as the housing and industrial estates.'

Catherine looked at him. 'You're not telling me Robert was involved in this?' She asked angrily.

'You know he wasn't. We wouldn't be in this mess if Robert had agreed at least to keep quiet. Fred Twilling had tried to bring him into his scheme several times. He must have told you this?'

Catherine ignored his last question; she had one of her own. 'And the last time Frederick Twilling tried to get Robert into this scheme was that morning wasn't it? The morning he claimed Robert had thumped him, the same day Twilling was murdered?'

'I had to suspend Robert. Don't you see? He was going to write to the Government Minister. He didn't know about Reede, but with Reede poking around your husband had to be discredited.' Mercer started to quiver.

Catherine realised her face betrayed that this was new and horrifying information. She was outraged at Mercer's activities. She wanted to tell the authorities – her sense of right and wrong could let her do nothing else. Yet she knew that now she was in the same position as Robert had been before he went missing. She knew about Mercer and Twilling. She had always despised her husband's superior but this was the first time she had ever feared him. She got up and made for the car.

'Catherine, wait!' called Mercer.

She stopped. She didn't look round.

'You can have the money that Robert would have got,' said Mercer. 'You must not talk to Reede. I'm finished with the Twillings. They use everyone. Think how useful that money would be for Laura and little Molly.'

"Good God, he would even sink to using my daughters to buy me off," thought Catherine. 'I hope Reede gets you all,' she answered. She started to walk over to the car as she continued, 'But you don't have to worry I won't tell anyone about all this. The way my husband has disappeared will be enough to keep me quiet.' It was a lie but she was already at the BMW. Catherine felt safe inside the locked car.

'What are you talking about? I don't have your husband,' said Mercer as he banged on the car window and pulled at the door handle.

Her blood was boiling and ready to say what she wanted: 'How can I believe you? You are scared of being caught and that is the only reason you are trying to stop your involvement with the Twillings. You could have killed Frederick and Kelvin Silverton for all I know. You tried to bribe me into silence. My Robert knew too much, and now he's gone.' She turned the key in the ignition. She steered the car away from Mercer. This took her in the opposite direction to the road, towards where the two rivers ran together. To get back on the road she would have to turn the car and drive past him.

What a burden Robert had carried. No wonder he had been sombre, thought Catherine. If only he had shared his misery with me, everything could have been so different.

She jammed on the brakes and stopped on the river bank. A thought cut across her mind: Jonathan Twilling hadn't asked her where her husband was even though he called him his father's murderer. Jonathan Twilling really could have murdered his father and his friend. He was certainly mad. Perhaps he performed a demented ritual where he called other people guilty to transfer his own guilt to them. Had he tried to get Robert to confess as he had tried to make her? Had Robert refused and Jonathan Twilling murdered him in a fit of temper? The thought jarred against her heart. No, she had already convinced herself that her husband was not dead. She would not change her mind.

But her mind twisted onto the slaughter of Frederick Twilling and Jonathan Silverton. Their murderer had put her into this tangle of dishonesty and she did not know whether it was Mercer, Jonathan Twilling, or somebody else. She even found herself considering Robert in that role. Kind, gentle Robert. She hated that her own thoughts had been corrupted. She wanted to kill that. "Please may Robert not have taken the right over life and death into his own hands," begged her aching heart and she aimed the thought at Mercer, followed by the car.

She was facing the stout grey man waving at her across the grass. She avoided looking directly at Mercer as she accelerated towards him.

# Chapter 13

The faces of the seated policemen and women were before Campbell, each one set with its own expression. They ranged from artificial attention and genuine enthusiasm through neutrality, to boredom, lethargy and irritability. The enthusiastic and irritable ones shuffled their chairs and feet while the others remained frozen in a tableau. The thought of being the focus of all their attention caused Campbell to pause awkwardly. He looked at the boards displaying photographs of the deceased, lists of dates with times next to them. They did not help him speak. Then he looked at the clock on the wall, quarter to five. The time acted as his prompt.

'We've been working on this case for three days now. Let's assess our progress and the information we have collected so far,' he said. His Edinburgh accent was very strong when he first spoke. It wasn't a cultured, clipped, almost English voice; it was the Edinburgh of the old tenement blocks from before the days of gentrification. He coughed into his hand and continued with his brogue softened. 'Our murderer has already struck twice and I think he will kill again. Our investigations urgently need to be resolved. I don't want another person to die in this way.

'I have no doubt that these murders were done by the same person as the modus operandi was identical and this information has continued to be withheld from the press. I say 'he' because I have considered the matter and the murderer would have to be strong to lift these bodies even though on both occasions lifting devices were used and the first victim was taken to the gantry in a wheelbarrow. It is also more likely that a man would have the necessary knowledge of the slaughtering process. Yes?' He said to Jenner who had her hand raised.

'I think I could lift one of those bodies, Sir. There are a lot of women

95

who, if angered, could produce an enormous amount of strength. There are also women butchers and vets.'

There was general tittering from the feet shufflers in the group and Jenner reddened.

'Point taken,' said Campbell with sufficient gravity to stop any more ridicule of the idea, but he put it to the back of his mind. It was far more likely to be a man, he decided and continued:

'Catherine Fenman has found both bodies and her husband, Robert Fenman, is missing. Robert Fenman had been accused by the first victim, Frederick Twilling, of hitting him and he had been suspended from work the same day Frederick Twilling was murdered. The second victim Kelvin Silverton was Catherine Fenman's ex-lover, motives for Robert Fenman to kill both men.' Campbell paused and looked into the eyes of each of the policemen and women assembled before him. They liked that story. He could see that. It was simple, straight forward, believable. 'So what have we got to back up this possibility?' he asked. There was no answer, he wasn't expecting one.

'Fenman has only the one car which his wife was driving,' he added. 'Robert Fenman arrived, apparently, at the Frederick Twilling murder site on a bicycle. He couldn't have put the equipment up in the morning when he had the car as he was otherwise engaged. He would have needed more transport than a bicycle to get the murder equipment there and set up. The hire car people have been checked. No-one remembers a Mr Fenman or anyone looking like him hiring a car in the two weeks prior to the murders. Local walkers in the area have stated that up until the day before the murder the woodland there was undisturbed and we have no witnesses for the day of the murder.'

Campbell nodded to Parnold and Parnold returned the gesture. 'Could he have borrowed a car?' the Inspector asked himself. 'Perhaps, the family friend, Mrs Sadie Groom may have leant him hers. That is a possibility we haven't checked. However it would have to have a bicycle rack fitted for that day and be big enough to get a wheelbarrow in it. Parnold, arrange for Mary Brown to go across and look at Sadie's car, will you.'

While Parnold made a note of this Campbell continued, 'The way Robert Fenman has disappeared is strange too. We've had appeals on the television and radio. This town is quite isolated. It's surrounded for ten miles with agricultural land and forest. No river boats have been reported stolen and a check on moored boats is still underway. He could have walked, of course, and the area is still being searched. We've checked the CCTV at the train stations and talked to staff. Or he might have used a car. Again this might point to borrowing a vehicle. Yes?' he asked WPC Garden whose hand was raised.

'Sir, yesterday, when I took Mrs Fenman around to Mrs Groom's, I had a word with Sadie Groom and she told me about Kelvin Silverton's visit to her house the night he was murdered.'

'Yes, I've seen your report. It has been most significant in building up the picture of events,' said Campbell.

The girl blushed. 'Her car was in her garage, Sir. She still had use of it.'

'Good,' said Campbell. 'At least we know that it hasn't gone missing at the same time that Robert Fenman went missing.'

She was the sort of girl who would always colour at praise, thought Campbell, and turned to the rest of the team. 'The murderer could have met Frederick Twilling close to the murder site. The victim was, however, drugged. How did we get on with that one Parnold?'

'Doctors may have it for use with violent psychiatric patients and, of course, the hospital also has supplies. They use it as a pre-med before an operation. They aren't aware of any thefts at the hospital, and we are still checking with the doctor's surgeries.'

'His mother-in-law is a doctor. Robert Fenman could have got it from her,' said WPC Jenner.

'That was the first place I checked this morning,' replied Parnold. 'I get the impression Dr Bane is not fond of her son-in-law. She wouldn't give him the time of day, let alone drugs. And when I checked at her surgery they said Dr Bane'd been off work for the last few weeks.'

'So if we assume Robert Fenman got hold of some of this stuff another way, injected Frederick Twilling with it, and put him in his wheelbarrow with his equipment.' He pointed at the photograph of the impression cast made in the forest. 'Do we have anything to back up this theory? Forensic says Fenman's clothes were only smeared with blood, not enough for them to be in direct contact with the victim at the time of his death. If he did do it he must have had overalls, knife, wellingtons to get rid of and, of course, the wheelbarrow. We haven't found anything in the area. He would have needed a car.'

'But he did use a car, the one his wife was driving. There needn't have been any sign of anything in the car if everything was wrapped in plastic.' Parnold sounded exasperated. 'She was in on it, she had to be.'

'Forensic are still looking at the Fenman's car. If they did it, why would they go and get help?' said Campbell.

'Because their car had run out of petrol. They couldn't get away quickly enough. They had to make it look right.'

'I think we'll have to double check Catherine Fenman's time table. We'll talk to her mother again,' said Campbell. 'The timing is very tight. We need some evidence, the murder weapon, clothing or confirmation from forensic that the wheelbarrow print comes from the Fenman's wheelbarrow.'

'He's missing. He's run away. That must be an indicator of his guilt,' said Parnold.

'He could've been taken or he could be dead,' remarked Campbell examining the movement in his wrist as he circled his hand to relieve a twinge. 'Whichever way we look at it, it is important that this man is found.' That's covered everything as far as Fenman's concerned, thought Campbell. 'Let's move on and look at other possibilities.' There were some surprised faces. Were there any other possibilities?

'Kelvin Silverton was also Twilling's solicitor, so there could be a connection with the business. There is another element we haven't looked at: the man that Mrs Catherine Fenman saw talking to Mercer and Frederick Twilling during the lunch time before Fred Twilling's death. We saw him at Jonathan Twilling's house. That dark blue car's been checked and I've spoken to Mercer. The extra man in the equation is Michael Reede. Yes?' He asked Jenner. Her hand was raised and her face was red. Unlike Garden, she was not inclined to blush, thought Campbell.

'There's been a Reede trying to reach you. He left his phone number. It's on your desk,' said WPC Jenner.

'Oh?' said Campbell with only mild concern.

'I'll get it,' she said leaving her front seat.

'Thank you,' said Campbell. There was no sarcasm or accusation in his voice, nor guilt that he should have found the note except for his persistent absenteeism from his office. He was just being polite. 'In the mean-time, we can study Frederick's relationship with his wife. It seems she was required to stay at home. Jonathan Twilling noticed this, but didn't care, while Sarah Twilling's son, Ernest Petry did care. Ernest is a butcher.'

'Ernest Petry's got alibis for both nights,' grumbled Parnold.

'Quite so,' agreed Campbell. 'And there is a family history of slaughtering their own meat. They had a shop here in Ouse Crossing.' He paused and raised his heels and balanced on the balls of his feet. 'There is also the position of the Middletons of Forest Cottage, where the Fenmans reported the murder to us. Are they telling the truth? Their son's also a butcher. He tells me his family felt fiddled out of their land by Frederick Twilling,' said Campbell.

'Mark Middleton also has alibis for both nights,' said Parnold.

Campbell paused, rubbed his wrist and continued, 'Yes, but it seems permission to develop a site has been turned down to the property owners until Frederick Twilling purchases the land. Then, hey-presto, he gets permission to build. If this is the case then anyone with a similar issue could have a motive for killing Kelvin Silverton and Frederick Twilling. We need to cross reference development applications, refusals and permissions given to Frederick Twilling over the last ten years. Something made this happen now.' He gestured at Parnold, and WPC Garden. 'You and you, get down to the Ouseland Council offices and check it out. We need a list of all the people who could have been aggrieved by Frederick Twilling by this activity.'

The self-closing door to Campbell's right opened. It was the same door Jenner had left by. She was returning. Some looked round; others looked pointedly in front of themselves. Campbell had intended to glance at her and then take Reede's phone number from her, but her face was agitated.

'What is it?' he asked her.

She held out two pieces of paper. The top one, Campbell could see had the name Michael Reede and a telephone number on it. He said something about being a private investigator. Campbell took the papers from her. 'And?' he asked.

'Sir, something's happened at Sadie Groom's house,' she replied. 'A neighbour has phoned to say the place has been left with the front door open.'

# Chapter 14

The BMW was barely a car's length away from Mercer before Catherine swerved past him.

She watched him through the rear view mirror standing alone between the two rivers, his jowls limp and his arms hanging by his sides. She dismissed any thought of Robert's guilt.

It was slow progress back to Sadie's with the traffic lights and road works. Catherine looked at the other travellers. They were piqued by a day's work and impatient from the belief that being as rude as possible to all other road users would get them home faster. Catherine smiled at them. Her attack on Mercer had eased her tension. She felt more in control of herself. She allowed cars into the stream of traffic from side roads. Something Robert always did, she remembered. And she cherished that thought, but thinking directly about him made her whole being ache as if a limb had been removed. She blinked hard and looked beyond the car windscreen.

She drove past buildings built in the nineteen sixties out of experimental materials and untried methods of construction. They were now covered by scaffolding and crawling with builders. Catherine noted from the builder's board that they were Frederick Twilling's employees. Their presence upset her so she turned and swore at a driver who appeared to be swearing at her for not moving when the traffic lights had turned green.

Beyond the lights she took a road on the right which took her down a narrower one edged with Victorian terraced houses. Streets of similar buildings ran down to her right. Her own home was along one of these. It was on the end of a terrace about half way down the road. The next street was Sadie's. Catherine passed the top of the road to enter the track beyond, which ran down the back gardens. She hadn't seen the pair of concrete gate posts at its entrance when she'd left Sadie's. She stopped. Why had it been easier getting out of this narrow opening earlier than it was to get back into it now, she wondered. Breathing deeply and counting she reversed, pulled wide found a forward gear, and passed Sadie's car between the concrete pillars.

Yes, this was Sadie's car. She had let her borrow it. How wrong she'd been about Sadie. Michael Reede, Sadie's friend or lover, was not a friend of the Twillings, but investigating them. So she had nothing to fear from her friend or Reede. But she felt a twinge of jealousy for her friend's closeness to another person. How she wanted Robert's comfort. Catherine released the seat belt and opened the car door. She could feel her perspiration chill in the outside air so she plucked at her dress pulling it away from her body, and she reached for her coat on the rear seat.

As she arrived at the garage doors a noise made her look up to the roof where she was confronted by a pair of disdainful feline eyes. She looked back down at the doors to find the padlock closed. Sadie had no doubt locked them after waving Catherine off that morning.

The back door to Sadie's house was locked too. There was no bell so she hammered on it with her fists and shouted her friend's name. She couldn't leave the car in the lane long as it was blocking the access to other people's garages and the garden allotments at the end. It wouldn't be long before people would want access.

Sadie's distorted image appeared behind the patterned glass of the back door. There was a large area of pink colour in the general shape of Sadie's dressing gown and a movement around the face area. It looked as though Sadie was rubbing sleep out of her eyes.

'The garage is locked,' Catherine called. She could hear gentle groaning and Sadie moved to one side of the glass. Sadie was weeping.

'Go away,' said Sadie.

'What's the matter?'

'You're the matter.'

'I'm sorry. I know this is all awful, but what can I do?'

'You've done enough to ruin my life. You being here has been enough.'

'I'll go, but tell me what has happened.'

'Michael's gone.'

'Who?'

'Michael Reede. He wouldn't stay because you've been here.'

'He's nothing to do with me,' said Catherine. 'Let me in. Everyone will hear us,' she pleaded.

Sadie opened the door. 'Michael Reede's everything to do with me,' she said, raising her voice. 'Well, he was until today. We were lovers. And I don't care who hears.'

'Michael Reede is a private investigator,' Catherine said tentatively, edging through the back door in to the kitchen.

'I know that,' said Sadie defiantly.

'Did you know he was working on corruption in the council?' Catherine kept her voice low and steady. 'He was investigating Mercer and the Twillings. He knows stuff that could put that lot where they belong: in jail. I need to know the details of what he's found out. I'm sure it will help me find Robert.' Catherine closed the kitchen door behind her as Sadie's voice rose again.

'You're daft. Robert isn't hiding from them. If he was frightened of them he'd have been in hiding for years. Michael cannot be compromised by being associated with friends of a murder suspect. There. Now you have it.'

'Is that what he said?'

'Yes,' confirmed Sadie.

'He'll come back.'

'He says not.'

'What about your husband?'

'He's not coming back either.'

'Oh, Sadie, I'm so sorry.'

'You don't have to be sorry for me. Look at your life!' And Sadie started to laugh manically. After a few moments it turned to equally violent crying. Catherine tried to touch her, but she pulled away.

'I hate you.' Sadie spat the words out at her. 'He just wanted to end it – us.'

'That couldn't be just because of me, Sadie.'

'He said it was.' Sadie started to tremble. 'Why shouldn't it be? Do you think there's something wrong with me?

'No, Sadie, of course not.' Catherine pushed past Sadie into the kitchen and put the BMW keys into the pot on the work top by the door. She made Sadie a cup of tea using a tea bag in a mug and ladling three heaped spoonfuls of sugar into its grey-brown depths. The milk splashed into the mug and onto the work top as she poured it into the tea. Catherine scraped a kitchen chair across the lino and lined it up with Sadie. She pushed her friend down into it and gave her the mug and ordered Sadie to drink. She watched her make grinding gulps as she did as she was told.

'You have to help me, Sadie. I need to find Robert.'

Sadie glanced up from her tea. Catherine could see that shock had started to set in.

Slamming the mug onto the draining board, Sadie said, 'Did you murder Michael? People seem to die wherever you go. I should never have asked you to stay. And where were you this afternoon? You could have killed Fred Twilling and Kelvin and Michael. And where is Robert? Did you do these filthy things together?'

'Michael's not dead, Sadie. You told me a moment ago that he left you.'

The woman had started to tremble, and tears flowed down her cheeks.

'Look,' said Catherine echoing her friend's over used word to get her attention, 'Calm down, Robert and I had nothing to do with any of this. You know that inside.'

A whimper came from upstairs. 'I'll get the twins down for you,' said Catherine.

'No, you won't,' said Sadie as if Catherine might harm them by her presence. Catherine watched her from the hall pull her long body up the stairs. When Sadie came down she was carrying her twins, one in each arm. They blocked her view of the steps. She stumbled on the bottom one and Catherine caught her elbow to steady her. The slender arm still wrapped around a child was pulled away.

'These murders are aimed at me in some way, Sadie. You and Michael are not involved.' Catherine's words were intended to calm Sadie. 'I was meant to find the bodies. Someone's trying to put the blame on me,' pleaded Catherine. 'I've had to hide my children away because I don't know what the danger is to them or where it will come from. Please Sadie, with Robert missing it's like there's a hole in my heart and my blood is leaking through it.'

Sadie put the twins in the living room by some toys and went into the kitchen to make the children a drink. She was sniffing and rubbing her eyes on her sleeve as she completed her task. She gave the boys their beakers and sat down on the settee near to them. The tears rolled down her face again. 'Look, Catherine, I know Michael would still be here if you hadn't stayed and he would have come back if Robert hadn't killed him.'

'Michael's only just gone. When he cools down he'll be back. Why should Robert want to kill Michael? He could have told him everything, all the things he was burdened with. Michael Reede would have been a friend for Robert, not an enemy.'

'Look, if he's so innocent, what makes you think Robert's still alive?' said Sadie smiling falsely through her tears at the twins.

'I know he is. Because I haven't found his body,' said Catherine. She hadn't realised the truth of this until she'd been goaded into saying it by Sadie. It shocked her. Death was so close. She felt she could almost touch her own death. But even closer than that was probable arrest and total separation from Molly, Laura and Robert for ever.

Sadie cringed. 'I'm going to phone the police. I'm going to tell them you murdered Michael.'

'No, Sadie, please don't.' Catherine remembered the fear in the eyes of the people at the cottage when Robert had asked them for help. They had pointed a gun at them.

She didn't know what to do. Catherine looked at the twins and couldn't help feeling relief that her daughters were out of this. Perhaps she ought to phone for help. Her steps were quick and determined as she went back into Sadie's hall. She didn't know who to phone. There was only Evelyn left. It wasn't until she picked up the phone that she changed her mind. She put the receiver down, the number not dialled. She went back into Sadie's front room and placed her hands on top of her friend's to gain the shocked woman's attention.

'Sadie, let's just go,' she said. She hoped her friend would come round from her conviction that Robert had killed Michael. Perhaps Sadie could really help her find Robert if she took her with her. She couldn't stay here, not like this. Not with Sadie saying such crazy stuff. The police might think her or Robert or both of them guilty for running away. But she wasn't running away, she told herself. She was going to look for Robert. She hoped he was missing from fear or from the misery she'd caused him and not because he'd been beaten to death by Jonathan Twilling, captured by Mercer or slaughtered by some other madman.

Sadie could no longer speak and Catherine couldn't tell her that she was worried the police might suspect her too. They had suggested that when they had spoken to her in hospital. And Sadie was in shock. Catherine would have to take her friend with her to protect her from the police, and that meant taking the infants as well. The two women were silent as Catherine put the twins in their suits and into their push-chair. She was surprised Sadie let her, yet she could see that her friend was losing touch with what was going on.

The operation seemed to be endless, and Catherine was sure there would be more people in the lane by now getting agitated by the blockage the BMW was making. In the kitchen she took biscuits automatically from a cupboard to keep the children happy as she fumbled in the pot for the car keys. 'Right, let's go,' she said regaining the BMW keys.

She opened the back door and lifted out the buggy. It was a tandem arrangement with one toddler seated slightly higher so by stretching his neck he could see over his brother. But now neither child was bothered about seeing as they were concentrating on their biscuits.

Sadie walked numbly. Catherine guided her by laying her own hand over her friend's on the handle of the buggy. Catherine feared for her life, half wondering if she wanted to preserve it, but knowing her daughters needed her because she'd needed her mother – a real mother, not that person who'd never loved her. The rhythm of her steps gave her strength. Robert had gone; there was nothing to keep her here. She couldn't believe he was able to come home now, whatever his reasons for going. So her resolve to disappear, to hide from the murderer and the policemen's prison, strengthened with each pace.

As they turned into the lane, Catherine heard a police siren in the distance. The two women and the push chair were making slow progress and panic was starting to thump in Catherine's chest. She tried to get Sadie to run, but her shocked steps could only plod. Catherine looked at Sadie and Sadie looked back. They were close and Catherine tried to focus on Sadie's eyes, but she could not find her friend inside them. The tall woman stopped. The last of her energy left her.

'Come on,' said Catherine pulling at the buggy. 'Let's get out of here.'

Sadie couldn't move, shock had slowly paralysed her. Uncertainty about Catherine's involvement had crippled her. Catherine saw this and knew she would have to leave her friend. She knew the police would find and question Sadie. She knew that would be a torturous experience, but her own disappearance would focus their thoughts on her and not her friend. She could not stay behind with Sadie. She could not risk arrest.

She looked at her lost friend. She said, 'Go inside', ran to the car and opened the door. As Catherine drove away she looked back and saw the twins jiffling in their push-chair seats. She said, 'Goodbye,' but her thoughts were with Molly and Laura. If she'd stayed and been arrested she knew her mother would not fight for her release. She would not even want to bring up her grandchildren. Catherine hated her mother for not loving her and more for not loving her grandchildren. Her instinct was to get them and hold them close, but her mind told her to leave them with Evelyn. They would be safer there while she looked for Robert.

# Chapter 15

Campbell had decided that Parnold, Jenner and Garden should come to Sadie's house and see what the fuss was about. He'd sent other members of his squad to the planning section of the council offices to investigate Frederick Twilling's business activities. Standing on the concrete apron to the garage, he looked down at Jenner's second piece of paper. It was a telephoned report of a disturbance at Sadie Groom's address from a Captain Ellis.

'There's no sign of Sadie Groom, her children, Catherine Fenman or her daughters,' said WPC Garden, having just returned from the house. She directed this comment at Parnold, but Campbell heard her.

WPC Jenner came forward. 'Inspector Campbell, Sir. We've taken statements from everyone who saw Sadie Groom, Catherine Fenman having an altercation in the back garden and Catherine Fenman leaving, which seems to be everyone in the street. This gentleman, Captain Enderby lives with Captain Ellis.'

'He has rooms in my house,' interrupted Captain Enderby.

'He says he saw what happened, but wants to speak to you himself.' WPC Jenner tutted at the gentleman with steel blue eyes and a handle bar moustache as she brought him from behind her.

'I was upstairs in my study, you understand,' said Captain Enderby. 'I have a medal collection up there, as I was just telling this young lady.'

The man seemed to be waiting for a prompt. It was Parnold who managed an, 'And?'

So Captain Enderby continued, 'I saw that gal who's been staying here arrive with Mrs Groom car. The garage seemed locked, so she went to get Mrs Groom. I said to myself there'd soon be a queue, and, indeed, Captain

Ellis turned up and couldn't get past. There were raised voices in the garden. My window was slightly ajar. They went inside for about half an hour and then they both came back out with the children. The odd thing is the guest got in Mrs Groom's car while Mrs Groom went off with the buggy and her little boys past all the jammed in cars. It was as if she didn't see them.'

'Who didn't see them?'

'Mrs Groom. The other woman in the car came by and asked everyone to back out. It was chaos. That's why we phoned the police.'

'Right, thank you Captain Enderby,' said Parnold. Campbell was suddenly aware of Parnold close to his left ear. 'Sadie Groom couldn't have gone far without a car,' whispered Parnold. There was satisfaction in his voice. Campbell flinched at it and looked directly at Captain Enderby.

'Earlier I was having a cup of tea in the back kitchen with Mrs Gibson,' Captain Enderby started but he was manoeuvred to one side by WPC Jenner. 'It's a funny business,' complained the Captain to Campbell. 'You police don't seem to want to know the facts. One of your lot interviewed Mrs Gibson from around the corner after that solicitor's death. She tried to tell your officers about it, but whenever she started to tell them about going after her lost cat no-one seemed to want to know.'

'We're very busy, Captain Enderby. I interviewed that woman. She'd spoken to Mrs Fenman just before Silverton's body was found,' said Parnold.

'What are you trying to get at, Captain?' asked Campbell.

'She saw something the night before. The night Silverton was murdered. You'll have to ask her. She knows.' With this Captain Enderby turned on the spot and marched away. Campbell caught WPC Jenner's expression of contained mirth at the Captain's high self-importance. Campbell didn't endorse it.

'Thank you, Captain,' said Campbell making the retreating military man pause. 'We will talk to Mrs Gibson immediately.' He turned to Jenner. 'Do you have her address?'

She nodded.

Campbell and Jenner left Parnold at the garage to continue finding out what had happened to Sadie and Catherine. Campbell wasn't sure if there was any problem to deal with or whether this was the kind of dispute that was best left for the parties involved to sort out themselves.

He and Jenner started to walk up the lane.

Garden came after them. 'Sir,' she said. 'I've just been notified that someone, a woman – she didn't leave her name – has phoned up and said that Catherine Fenman has murdered a Michael Reede.'

'Where and when?' asked Campbell steadily.

'She didn't say.'

'Could you recognise Sadie Groom's voice?'

'I think so.'

'I think you ought to go back to the control room and have a listen. Just see if it is her.'

'Jenner, pop back and see Parnold. Tell him we need to look around for a body. Get that garage open for a start.'

At the top of the lane the large white van of the forensic department was parked across the concrete pillars, blocking the access. The allotment gardeners seemed to have given up on the day's endeavours. Mary Brown's ample white boiler suited posterior could be seen as she leaned into the back of the vehicle.

'Afternoon?' Campbell asked. 'I can't say it's a good one though, not with murders being reported more frequently than I get breakfast. What brought you here today? We have only just been told that we need to look for a body.'

Mary replied. 'I got a call to look at Sadie Groom's car so came by. As I was in the area I returned the Fenman's wheelbarrow.'

'Sadie Groom's car's not here. Catherine Fenman's driven it away.' Campbell'd walked on barely expecting a reply. He was already several paces past the vehicle when Mary Brown called to him:

'Oh, Campbell. Don't you want to know, dear? The tyre markings on Fenman's wheelbarrow were the same pattern as the ones found at Frederick Twilling's murder, but when they were looked at in detail, wear markings etc, it wasn't the same tyre. We've traced the manufacturer. I'm afraid they were a common type and can be found on several different makes of wheelbarrow.' Mary Brown smiled warmly and banged the back door of the van shut.

WPC Jenner had caught up with Campbell as he was talking to Mary Brown. She decided that Mrs Gibson smiled like a rat inspecting poisoned bait as the woman poked her head out of her front door, and when she explained why they'd come her face changed into an expression of rodent like satisfaction.

'I thought you lot would be back,' she said.

The room they were taken into was brown. The woodwork was chocolate coloured, the curtains were beige with white and brown daisies, the walls were coffee coloured. Even the carpet was beige with brown swirls across it. Mrs Gibson sat on the settee. This was also brown, and had a beige check. Against one wall was a large sideboard covered in cat ornaments. There was a living cat on each of the two dining chairs in the room and one on one of the two chairs of the checked three piece suit. Another cat covered the other half of the settee Mrs Gibson was sitting on. The acrid smell of used cats' trays nipped Jenner's nostrils.

WPC Jenner took the remaining seat and watched Campbell raise himself onto his toes, lower himself and then rock back onto his heels as he stood by the door.

'Stand still, can't you?' Mrs Gibson demanded of the police inspector. He stopped mid-sway. She pulled the cat next to her on to her lap, cuddled it, kissed it and then puckered her lips to push a slurred endearment at the animal. 'Horace is always getting lost, see.' She put the cat down on her knee. 'That woman, Mrs Fenman was so rude to me.'

'We need to know what you know, Mrs Gibson,' said Campbell. 'You told Captain Enderby you saw something the night before the body was discovered.'

'Yes, I was looking for my cat. He'd been missing all day and then he was missing all that night too. I can guess what he was up to, mind.' She winked at WPC Jenner. The policewoman half smiled and Mrs Gibson continued, 'I was up that alley that runs along the back of the Fenman's house. Most people along there have high fences so you can't see in the gardens, but they have low gates, so, if you lean over you can have a good look round.'

'Did you see something in one of the gardens, then, Mrs Gibson?' asked WPC Jenner.

'No, love. But I'd just pulled back from leaning over one of the gates and I saw a car go by the top of the alley.'

'That isn't unusual, surely?' asked Campbell. Jenner saw Mrs Gibson give him a look of complete disdain.

'Not in itself, but it kept coming by and slowing, nearly to a stop,' said Mrs Gibson.

'Did you recognise the car?' asked WPC Jenner.

'I don't understand cars really. It wasn't a Rolls and it wasn't a Mini. All the cars look the same to me these days. To tell you the truth I thought it was Mr Fenman's car 'cause I'd just given up on Horace and I met him at the top of the lane.'

'Was it a saloon or an estate car?' asked Campbell.

'You mean a shooting break thing? No it wasn't one of them. Hatch back, I think you call 'em.'

'What colour was it, Mrs Gibson?' asked WPC Jenner.

'What, dear?' asked Mrs Gibson playing with her cat.

'The car, Mrs Gibson.'

'I couldn't tell you. Those yellow street lights change the colours so much. Isn't that right, dear?'

Jenner nodded and started to move towards Inspector Campbell while keeping her body facing Mrs Gibson. From there she and her boss edged their way back to the front door followed by a volley of information about Horace's love life.

'That was just about a waste of time,' said Jenner once safely outside. 'We know it couldn't have been Fenman's car, because we had that. And her information is unreliable.'

'She saw Mr Fenman there though. The last positive sighting before he disappeared,' said Campbell. 'And Silverton's car was a Volvo estate, so it wasn't his car she saw. It all helps, Constable.' Jenner looked at him hard trying to read his face. It was impossible. He was looking at the darkening sky. She readied herself for an original reply to his expected comment about the weather, but he never got a chance to make it.

Parnold's car stopped next to Campbell. The Inspector bent down when he was called and looked across the empty passenger seat into the back. WPC Garden was sitting in the back with Sadie Groom and her twin boys.

'We found her wandering the streets, Inspector,' explained Garden. 'I never got back to the radio room. We're going to take her to the hospital. She seems to be in shock.'

'Has she told you anything?' asked Campbell. He noted how grey Sadie Groom looked and the fidgeting toddlers.

'Only that she wants to die and Catherine Fenman's name,' replied Garden.

Without warning, Sadie Groom turned to WPC Garden and gripped her arm so that the fabric of the policewoman's sleeve contorted and twisted underneath her grasp. 'Catherine took my car. She left me. Michael's left me. Everyone's left me.'

'Michael who?' asked Garden.

'Michael Reede.' Sadie's voice faded away and her eyes focussed themselves on some distant object. 'Catherine's murdered him.'

Campbell addressed Parnold, 'We've got the details of Mrs Groom's car?'

'Yes, Sir.'

'We need to speak to Catherine Fenman. Make sure everyone knows we are looking for her and what vehicle she's in.'

'Constable,' this time he was addressing Jenner, 'Take Mrs Gibson for a walk to a car park and see if she can pick out a car like the one she saw the night Kelvin Silverton was murdered.'

For a moment Campbell watched Parnold and Garden drive off towards the hospital with WPC Jenner standing beside him. He flexed his left arm at the elbow and rubbed it with his right hand. 'Horace is a strange name for a cat,' he observed.

'Is anything wrong, Sir?' asked Jenner.

'My elbow keeps clicking,' he said.


Campbell heard Parnold complain to WPC Jenner the next morning. Campbell had looked at his desk and, as it had been covered with reports, he had picked up a pile of statements to take to the car park. Jenner replied to Parnold that Mrs Gibson could hardly tell the difference between a car and a motorbike let alone between different models, and as for her idea of colours... Campbell closed the office door behind him.

He was already sifting through his papers in the passenger seat when Parnold came and sat next to him. Campbell could sense the excitement coming off his body.

The young man spoke in a rush: 'The field next to, you know, that head of development man, Mercer? It was recently bought by Frederick Twilling. He hadn't applied for planning permission, but another company who'd owned the land previously had had an application turned down to turn the site into a gravel pit. We've just got the report from the lot that went to the council offices yesterday.'

'What sort of car has he got?' asked Campbell gently.

'A Citroen.' Parnold seemed to pause for dramatic effect. Campbell sighed, so the young man said, 'His wife, Susan, has a car like the Fenman's.

Same colour, everything.'

'The Mercers have an alibi for Frederick Twilling's murder.'

'It's hardly water tight and Mercer doesn't have one for Kelvin Silverton's death.

Campbell said, 'O.K. Let's go.'

'I checked,' said Parnold. 'Mercer is still at home. He hasn't returned to work.'

'Ah,' said Campbell. It was almost an agreement to visit Mercer or so Parnold seemed to think because he started the car.

'Take me back to the hospital, Sergeant,' said Campbell. 'I want to speak to Susan Mercer. I wonder if she had just finished her evening shift when Mrs Gibson saw that car.'

There she was. Campbell recognised her as the nurse who'd told him Robert Fenman had gone for a cup of tea. Her tidy body made the blue checked garment she wore seem attractive and her legs looked shapely against the flat shoes. Or perhaps it could be that he was getting tired and his defences were down. He coughed and settled himself to the interview. He could feel Parnold almost quivering beside him.

Her soft smile faded as Campbell started to question her about her husband's movements. She confirmed the chip shop queue and his visit to his mother. She even took them to see the old woman.

'Would you have access to this chemical?' Campbell passed her the chemical name carefully transcribed across one page of his note book as they walked down the ward.

'No more than any other nurse who administers pre-meds before operations,' she replied. She passed him back his notebook. He noted her face sharpen.

'What time did you leave yesterday?' he asked.

'Late. About midnight. I worked over-time. It was busy. What is all this about, Inspector?'

'Do you have any connection with the local abattoir, Mrs Mercer?'

'What a funny question. Is someone drugging the animals down there?'

'They stun them before they kill them, Mrs Mercer, with electricity or a captive bolt pistol,' said Parnold. His body tensed like a terrier watching a rabbit hole.

'I know that. My brother is the manager. He hasn't said anything about problems down there. That's why we moved this way when we got married so I could be near my family. He's all I've got.' Her face relaxed slightly.

'Wendling?' asked Parnold. 'Didn't he mention to you that we'd been round?'

'No, should he?' she snapped back.

Campbell laid his hand on Parnold's arm. 'Not yet,' he said. 'Thank you, Mrs Mercer, you've been most helpful,' he added.

'Arrest her,' spluttered Parnold when they reached the car park.

'Not enough,' said Campbell his Edinburgh accent hanging onto the words. 'Their alibi for Frederick Twilling's murder still stands.'

'His mother!' scoffed Parnold. 'We can get the rest out of Mrs Mercer with questioning.'

'They were in public places. We can check that out later. I want to see Donald Mercer.' Campbell rocked back and forth on his heels and toes while he waited for the Sergeant to unlock the car.

'Mercer could be hiding the Fenmans,' said Parnold suddenly sounding very Norfolk. 'That cottage is right out of the way. If Susan Mercer ha'n't tipped him off.'

Campbell was momentarily perplexed: whatever would Mercer want with hiding the Fenmans? Mercer had suspended Robert Fenman and it was obvious Fenman didn't like Mercer. He sucked the side of his thumb which he'd just sliced on a sharp piece of paper and turned his full attention to his Sergeant.

'Mercer would be the ideal accomplice to Robert Fenman,' said Parnold. 'His wife has access to drugs at the hospital. He knew Frederick Twilling and Michael Reede and I expect he knew Silverton. And now we know his brother-in-law just happens to be the manager of the local slaughterhouse.' By this time their car had reached the forest along the Hillvill road.

Campbell glanced towards the site of Frederick Twilling's murder. 'Wendling was a pleasant sort of man. He had a pride in his work but he did say when asked he didn't know how to slaughter, his skills were managerial.'

'He probably lied.'

'You favour a Mercer-Fenman conspiracy?' asked Campbell. He tried not to sound amused. Parnold had talent, and all views in a case were worth looking at, but this one he could not take seriously. The men despised each other. 'OK, so let's assume Mercer's alibis don't add up. It's possible that Mercer could be the murderer full stop. End of story.'

'When I got Mercer's story out of him yesterday evening for the Silverton murder, he was unnaturally helpful,' said Parnold, raising his eyebrows. Campbell felt the implication in his voice that he didn't think Campbell ever read reports.

'You left me a report. Good work,' said Campbell meaning, "Of course I read the reports I'm given. You think I'm useless, don't you? Well, it takes years to gain the experience which gives the feel for what's wrong and the instinct to see a genuine lead." His thumb started to throb so he sucked at the wound while Parnold completed the journey to Mercer's cottage.

Mercer was in his garden in thick suede protective gloves and wellingtons. His brown corduroy trousers and green quilted vest gave him the look of a country gentleman. Only his stiffness as he piled old raspberry canes and hedge trimmings onto a bonfire with a garden fork indicated to Campbell that this was something Mercer was not used to doing. And from the size of the bonfire he'd been busy some time.

Without remembering how he'd got from the car to inside the gate, Campbell found himself looking amiably around the garden. It contained a double garage, a small garden shed and a greenhouse, which looked new. In the flower garden a few roses had found the energy to bloom again. An area set aside for vegetables had parsnips and leeks standing in neat rows.

'Hard work?' Campbell asked Mercer.

'My wife likes a traditional garden. She usually does most of the work, but I thought I'd have a go. There's something about a bonfire, cleansing, life's cycle of ashes, man's mastery of flame. How can I help you?' Campbell studied the man's changed attitudes. Mercer caught his eye and said, 'I'm sorry about the other day. The murders had frightened me. Your accusations had frightened me. I feel better now.'

Campbell noted that the way Mercer talked meant that the words 'I' and 'me' were heavily emphasised. It made the man sound self-centred. Yet his explanation was not enough to cover his change of mood. There was almost a religious fervour in his speech.

'I believe your brother-in-law works in the slaughterhouse?' enquired Campbell.

'What do you want with him? He's as harmless as a fly. He can't even cope with the animals being killed.'

Campbell decided to try another angle. 'You told us about Fenman's argument with Frederick Twilling. You know he's still missing?'

'I saw it on the news. They were saying Mrs Fenman was missing too,' said Mercer. 'I spoke to her just before she disappeared, but you know.' He nodded to Parnold, and asked, 'Whatever frame of mind must that poor woman be in?'

'What did she say?' asked Campbell.

'She said she was fed up with the police.' Mercer shifted his feet and looked away.

Campbell shook his head as if absorbing this quandary. He spoke slowly as he said, 'I believe Frederick Twilling had just purchased this field next to your cottage before his death.'

Mercer lost his healthy radiance immediately. His face looked rough and the skin around his eyes darkened. He turned away and forked more brush onto his bonfire. 'He didn't care who he trod on. But I didn't kill him.'

'Your statement about your whereabouts leaves plenty of loose time that has yet to be accounted for,' said Parnold. 'And, you have no alibi for Silverton's death.'

'Can you say you are with someone every minute of every day, Sergeant?' asked Mercer. 'It isn't me you need to see about murdering Frederick Twilling. It's that son of his. He's as mad as his mother was. And he's corrupt. He's been screwing his father out of money for years. Perhaps he wanted the pile that was coming all to himself...' His voice tailed off.

'Pile of money?' queried Campbell.

'Yes,' agreed Mercer. 'You might as well know. I didn't tell Catherine Fenman this. I tried to tell her. I was pulling out from the Twillings' schemes. When money isn't easy to come by and land isn't in demand it's cheap and the Twillings buy it up. There's nothing wrong with that, of course. That's what property dealers do. Even before he married Sarah Petry I'd known Twilling to hang on to land for fifteen years.' Mercer looked around anxiously and added, 'I wasn't going to have anything to do with it, and the Twillings said they could do it without my help.'

'What?' asked Parnold.

'Fix the area plan for the next ten, fifteen and twenty years. Arrange the development areas to be allocated to land they already own. Land they bought at agricultural prices. Believe me; Frederick Twilling had enough contacts and friends to do it, even at a national level.'

'He still needed you,' said Parnold.

'Not really,' said Mercer.

'You didn't say this before,' said Parnold. His ears were red and his gaze demanding. 'It's only because Reede's been poking about and connected you all up you're coming clean now.'

'If you think Reede is a good man, think again,' retorted Mercer.

'You wanted out, but Frederick Twilling wouldn't let you, so you killed him,' accused Parnold. 'You could have killed Silverton for similar reasons. Do you know where Reede is? Is he dead because he knew all about you? Did you kill him?'

'No. No. No.' With each denial Mercer thumped his garden fork into the ground. When he looked up he was calm again. 'Originally I became a planner because I wanted to work for the community. I'm not the sort of man who kills. I'm off work now because I cannot handle the grief from these deaths.'

'You mean, you can't handle the situation you have put yourself in,' said Parnold. Mercer fell across his spade and wept.

Campbell thanked Mercer for his co-operation and took Parnold by the arm and steered him back to the car. He was pleased with the result of the interview. He was pleased that Parnold had behaved like the terrier he was and worried the truth out of the man. Now it was time to put him back on his leash.

'Aren't we going to arrest him for corruption?' asked Parnold.

'The whole matter amounts to a separate investigation,' said Campbell. 'We will have to get Fraud Squad onto that one. This man is not our murderer. It is clear he has no idea that the victims have been slaughtered like pigs. He was totally open-faced when he was telling me about his brother-in-law, Wendling – so was his wife, for that matter.' Campbell asked, 'Have we found out yet who Reede was employed by, and what he had found out?'

'We checked with his office. They said he was on leave. They had nothing to do with his present investigation,' replied Parnold, carefully taking back his arm.

Campbell cast his mind over the situation. He had so much information, yet the murderer seemed as far from arrest as when he first saw Frederick Twilling's body.

Campbell went back to Mercer. He was where he'd left him.

'If you are untying yourself from the Twillings this is the time to tell us what you know.'

'I've told you everything.'

'No, you haven't. Reede knows more, doesn't he?'

'He's not going to go to the authorities with what he knows. I am. I don't know who Reede was working for, but I think he has gone in with Jonathan Twilling now. Jonathan's already taken on a heavy into his new set-up. Find Jonathan and you'll find Reede.'

'You'll go down with it,' said Campbell.

'I know,' said Mercer. 'I should have stopped this a long time ago.'

'Your wife will be home soon. Do you want me to phone her?'

'It's alright I'm not going to do anything stupid.'

Campbell turned and left.

Every time he thought he was getting close to the murderer, the investigative path twisted away in another direction. It was like walking along the bottom of the glen at Campbell's Castle. He'd been there once with Margaret. He denied any fine feelings towards the building despite all its splendid architecture. They'd taken careful steps all the way. Foaming water pushed downhill, changing its route to the easiest path making the mossy rocks slippery, as he and Margaret travelled upwards towards the castle. Yet when they arrived they'd laughed at the fact that they'd not taken the easy made-up route from the car park. An incongruously pleasant memory – he closed it off.

He feared he'd missed something. And, worse though, was his feeling that the murderer's madness was reaching its climax. He had to stop it.

Back at the car Parnold asked him, 'Where to next?'

'Jonathan Twilling's house,' Campbell replied.

# Chapter 16

Catherine had watched the police come to her mother's house and her childhood home from Sadie's car. She'd parked it in a copse just over the road from there. No doubt, the police were searching for her, she thought. And she'd seen them leave. That was the second time that they'd called while she'd been watching from her vantage point. They'd called yesterday as well.

As she guessed that the police would be looking for her in Sadie's car she hadn't dared to drive around and look for Robert. While the wind blew off the fens all night rocking the trees she'd slept on the back seat. When she'd awoken her skin felt tacky inside her clothes and she was cold from her centre through to her extremities.

But it had been worth it to continue her watch over the front of her mother's house. She had to wait until she thought it was safe to go over and fetch Molly and Laura. There had been little to see after her mother had shown the police officers off the premises for the second time. She hadn't seen her children, which made her anxious. But she told herself she was being silly and they would be out the back, in the green house or reading one of Evelyn's many books in their bedroom.

She longed for their softness and warmth, the clattering chatter from Molly and the nearly adult conversation from Laura. She wanted to touch them, to hold them. Her gaze searched Evelyn's house and garden again.

As evening fell again she saw George drive out of the garage in his white car. The mist was rising and it swirled around making the pale vehicle look ghost like as it moved apparently wheel-less from the drive.

Catherine toyed with the idea of walking across to her mother's and leaving Sadie's car hidden in the copse. But she wanted to take Laura and

Molly with her and they wouldn't get far without a car. She knew her mother would not lend her anything let alone a car. So she drove Sadie's car out from the undergrowth by the copse, down a short tractor track and out into Tonne Road. The turning into Evelyn's driveway was almost immediately on her left.

Evelyn's next door neighbour's 'For Sale' sign had been knocked down over part of the drive. She managed to avoid it as, no doubt, George had done. She was pleased he was not there. She didn't want to involve him in this.

She looked at her mother's square house. She hated it. It was like a hole in space, a blackness in the darkness of evening. Perhaps she should have come here earlier, but she knew her mother. Evelyn would not have lied to the police to hide her daughter. At least now she had already dismissed the police with her honest sounding voice and business-like manner.

Well, thought Catherine, I'm here and I'm not going to be manipulated by my mother this time. She looked again at the house. It was wrong. The blackness of the building had purple areas indicating the position of the windows. Now she was walking close to them she could see it wasn't because the heavy velvet curtains were drawn cutting out the electric light to the outside world, but because the curtains had not been drawn and there were no lights on in the room.

She felt on edge from all the waiting and the wanting of her children. She wanted their happy noise, instead there was a stillness that equated with emptiness. There was no longer any Kimber to bark and both the front and back doors were locked. She banged at each in turn, screaming her daughters' and her mother's names time and time again. It was not madness. She knew that. But something inside her felt that by calling their names she could create their beings out of the nothingness. She stopped and rested her buzzing head against the back door. She felt an arm slip through hers. It felt like a stranger's.

'Don't cry, dear.' It was her mother. Such intimacy was alien between them. It felt false. Worse than false.

Catherine pulled back her arm. 'Where are my children?' she asked. She searched her mother's eyes. They were patronising. They told her nothing. She repeated her question, but her mother's grip became firm.

'Catherine, come with me,' said Evelyn. The older woman walked at a funereal pace away from the house and down the garden. Level with the apple trees there was a recently formed gap in the hedge.

Catherine stopped. She had a feeling of dread creeping into her stomach. 'What's going on?' she asked.

'Go through here and you'll see,' said her mother pushing her through the gap. There was a square flat roofed building on the other side of the hedge. The brickwork was painted white and reflected the small amount of light from the moon. 'Catherine, we'll be safe from the police here,' said Evelyn smiling.

Catherine had always had difficulty understanding her mother but now she didn't know her at all.

# Chapter 17

Jonathan Twilling made a wild groaning sound and clutched his stomach when confronted by Campbell. Then he crumpled down into a crouch and rocked back on his heels until the curve of his back was against his car.

'We know you were fiddling your father,' said Campbell.

Jonathan Twilling started to cry. It was a moaning, gulping sound. Campbell watched him. They were in Jonathan Twilling's driveway.

After a moment the young man started to speak in a tight gasping voice. 'I didn't want my father to die,' he said. 'He was so mean. He made my mother's life a misery. He took her dignity away from her. He was rude to her in front of people. He put her down all the time, until she felt like nothing. Then when she was a snivelling heap he shoved her off to an institution, said she was ill. I hated him for that, but he had no feelings. No-one could hurt him emotionally. I tried to but I just got screwed up. I wanted to kill myself, I even tried once, but he didn't care. Oh, hell, I miss my mother. Why did he have to take her away?'

Campbell didn't say anything, knowing that the young man's sobs were only a pause in his outpourings.

'I wanted him to suffer. He only cared about money and power. Those were the things he would miss. Kelvin Silverton understood what I wanted to do, and he had the perfect scheme. We found the land owners and handled the sales. He didn't check. In another ten years the old man would have wondered where all the money had gone, and where I'd gone too. Greedy Bastard. Dying was too easy for him.' Jonathan Twilling's fair hair was darkened by sweat in the cold night air. Campbell touched him on the arm.

'Reede had found out about the land deals,' said Jonathan Twilling. 'He knew how Father was working the planning system.'

'You had good reason to kill your father. You could have killed Silverton so you could keep all the money to yourself, or perhaps he would no longer give you an alibi for your father's murder. And, where is Reede? Is he dead? He could put you all in prison,' said Campbell with a slight frown and a soft searching tone in his voice. 'Did you kill them, or have them killed, Mr Twilling?' he asked.

'Kill who?' asked Jonathan Twilling.

Campbell could see the young man's eyes were not registering even that he was a policeman. The words Jonathan had spoken were not in evidence to a policeman, but an offloading of his burden of guilt, hate and grief. Campbell wanted to ask him who Reede was working for, but he knew this would be a waste of time. Jonathan's thoughts were incoherent. He had to get him thinking unemotionally, but not yet. He went back to his original question. In the young man's present babbling state he would confess to anything he had done, so he reminded him of the confirmed victims' names, 'Your father, Frederick Twilling, and Kelvin Silverton. Did you kill them or have them killed?'

'I didn't kill them or have them killed,' he replied. 'I wanted to kill my father, but I couldn't. That's why we were systematically taking his money. And I would never have killed Kelvin. I loved him like a brother.' Then he continued, 'I wanted to eliminate Reede, but I feared his intelligence.'

Campbell, who'd been crouching down on his haunches next to Jonathan Twilling, stood up carefully, straightened his back and looked up briefly. His gaze returned to the man at his feet as Jonathan pushed choking sounds out of his throat and banged the back of his head against the car.

'Reede found out you were fiddling your dad. Mercer thinks he came to work for you. Is that likely after what he found out about you? Have you killed him?' He asked the crucial question again.

'He does work for me now, yes. I haven't killed him.' Jonathan recovered a little and stood up. He still leaned against his car.

'Where is he?' asked Campbell.

'Reede's not here. He's with his new girl-friend,' replied Jonathan, wiping the back of his hand across his mouth.

'Who is she?'

'A vet over Hillvill way, Rebecca Haricotte.'

Campbell made a note and changed tack to the last remaining missing person. Perhaps Jonathan Twilling could resolve that one too. 'And what about Robert Fenman? What do you know about him?'

'He's a goody-goody.' Jonathan Twilling sneered. Campbell noticed the sudden defensive jut of his jaw.

'Do you think he's dead?' asked Campbell heavily.

'Well, I haven't killed him if that's what you mean – or had him killed. And, I don't know where he is either before you start accusing me of something else. I can tell you one thing though: he hasn't got it in him to kill a man.'

Campbell didn't judge Jonathan's expertise at criminal psychology worth commenting on but he thanked him for his time and left him making his way unsteadily back into his house. The Fraud Squad would deal with him.

Reede answered Rebecca's door wearing only a towel around his waist. Jenner thought that Reede must think himself to be more attractive than he actually was.

'Can I help?' he asked with a swagger.

Campbell made the introductions and invited himself and Jenner in. He followed with, 'You've been phoning us. You left your number, but you haven't been answering it just lately. We traced your car number and you weren't at your home address.'

'Oh no, so I haven't. It was a mistake any way. I didn't need to talk to you guys after all. And as you can see I'm safe and well here.'

'You've been investigating Jonathan and Frederick Twilling, I understand?' asked Campbell.

'No, mate. You've got that wrong,' replied Reede.

'Jonathan Twilling told me you were working for him now.'

'He's a good bloke,' said Reede.

'He's a bloke, who had his fingertips in his father's business interests before he died and now he has all his father's business,' Campbell tweaked the word 'bloke' as if it were alien to his vocabulary.

'Look,' said Reede, 'can I get some clothes on?'

'I don't see why not.' Campbell paused long enough for the man to don shirt and trousers and then called out. 'What did you think of Frederick Twilling?'

'Jonathan wanted to know more about him. I told him what he wanted to know. That Frederick Twilling had it coming to him.' Reede came back in dressed in jeans and t-shirt.

'And did you give it to him?' Again Campbell sounded as if he were carefully speaking in a foreign tongue.

'Course not,' scoffed Reede. 'You think it was just the planning stuff Frederick was in to. Well, old Freddy was a builder, you know. He got all the council's building contracts without any competition from others. Oh yes, little miss, I can see your disbelief.'

Jenner cringed at the patronising look he gave her.

Reede continued, 'They have systems to prevent such things: all fair and above board. Not! Frederick Twilling became untouchable. That sort of man deserves all he gets.'

'You sound very angry, Mr Reede. Did you kill Frederick and his solicitor, Kelvin Silverton?' Campbell's squirrel stoop straightened to give more effect to his height. 'To get in with Jonathan?'

'No, I didn't.' Reede stared at them without guile. 'But I will tell you that the council has a big black hole where there should be tax payer's money and it doesn't take an idiot to see who's got all the cash.'

'Did they realise what you were up to?'

'No. They were flattered to have a profile done by a journalist for a national newspaper.'

'Are you a journalist?' asked Jenner. She wondered if pretending to be a journalist counted as a crime. She hoped so, but doubted it somehow.

'No, poppet, I'm a private Dick. Or didn't you get that one?'

'How long have you and Rebecca been going out?' asked Campbell clearly ignoring the sharp looks being exchanged between Jenner and Reede.

'Two days,' said Rebecca walking in and offering her hand to Campbell.

'I understand you're a vet?' he asked.

'Small animals, the smaller the better,' replied Rebecca, her Dublin accent almost kissed the air when she spoke.

'Have you ever worked in a slaughterhouse?'

'I'm a vegetarian,' explained Rebecca, 'so I did a minimal amount of visits to the slaughterhouse itself as a student. It was more observation than hands on stuff. Why do you ask?' She tucked a strand of brunette hair behind her ear.

'No particular reason, Miss Haricotte,' said Campbell, looking down at his feet. 'How did you two meet?'

'I ran over a cat. I took it into the vets,' interrupted Reede.

'Where?' asked Jenner.

'Just round the corner from here.'

'Mrs Sadie Groom seems in a distressed state,' added Jenner looking at Miss Haricotte. Rebecca Haricotte looked confused.

'What's that to me?' asked Reede.

'Thank you for your time Mr Reede and Miss Haricotte.' Campbell brought the interview to a close.

'No bother,' said Rebecca smiling and closing the door behind them as they left.

'Stay lucky!' called Reede.

Jenner was seething. 'You let them get off light,' she complained. 'She's a vet and he's a Dick.'

'Thank you, Jenner. I don't like Mr Reede either but I don't think either Mr Reede or Miss Haricotte has killed anybody.'

Jenner gave Campbell a side long look and wondered where Reede had run over the cat. Even that wasn't illegal.

'I need to think,' he said.


Campbell looked over the scene of Frederick Twilling's death. The plastic ribbon was loose and dangling. It looked like the end of a party when the paper streamers have turned into litter and the noise is no longer cheerful.

'Why's he brought us back here?' grumbled WPC Garden, leaning against a tree. 'Mary Brown's been here and got everything. The hottest clues, I would have thought, would have been with the latest victim. And I'm hungry.'

'Inspiration,' said WPC Jenner. 'He's feeling the vibrations from the soil. Dead men's blood talks.'

Campbell heard them, but did not care what they said. He was still like a squirrel listening. Parnold was rooting about in the darkened forest like a Jack Russell. The air was chilling rapidly so that small spirals of condensing moisture came from their mouths as they spoke. The trees seemed to be swallowing the light. He saw Parnold stumble. The circular paths they'd each taken from the murder site had brought them back to within a few feet of each other. Campbell crouched on the ground and moved pieces of bark around on the floor.

'I'm not sorry I brought you out here. I want you to visualise the murder, in fact, the murderer,' he said. 'Let's take Catherine Fenman's story as true. That leaves us with a drugged body taken to this site in a wheel barrow, hoisted to this gantry and having its throat slit.'

'It was Frederick Twilling,' said Garden, sucking her lip thoughtfully.

'It would have needed someone very strong, a man,' said Parnold.

'No, I don't think so,' said Jenner. 'With a wheel barrow someone small can lift quite heavy weights. Remember the gantry was fitted with a pulley. This was a calculated murder by someone who was not that strong.'

Mist was rising from the undergrowth hiding their feet. Garden shivered. 'We can see all this in the office.'

'I agree, but we can't feel it there,' said Campbell.

'Both the Fenmans are missing,' said Parnold to Campbell. 'You, yourself, said that Robert Fenman was no athlete.'

'Neither of the Fenmans are slaughterers. We've seen that the victims were killed with techniques used in an abattoir,' said Campbell. 'The Petry lad and young Middleton are butchers, despite having alibis and little chance of getting hospital drugs. The girl friends work in a dress shop. That was in one of the reports. And, Jonathan Twilling, could he use techniques learnt in a slaughter house?'

'One of his builders might have the skills but a strong man wouldn't need all this gear,' said Jenner.

'But he might want to use it,' suggested Parnold.

'Jonathan denied murdering or getting someone else to murder his father and Kelvin.' Campbell sighed. 'It is all a soup of possibilities.'

'Can we go home, I'm cold?' asked Garden rubbing her shoulders briskly.

Campbell sent Parnold, Garden and Jenner back to the track that held Parnold's car. Four days ago the murderer would have parked there and returned, after killing Frederick Twilling, by that same path, through the forest pushing the empty wheelbarrow. He had already checked again the track where the murderer had parked the car. It was firm and dry. It held no secrets, so Campbell chose to walk to the road reversing the route Catherine Fenman and her husband had claimed they'd taken to the murder site. When he reached the main road he glanced along it.

Yesterday they'd held a reconstruction of Fred Twilling's last walk. So far nothing worthwhile had come of it. It seemed no-one had seen him that night between the time his son had seen him outside his house going towards the forest and his death.

"This road's never very busy at that time of night, but surely someone would have seen him," thought Campbell.

He turned and trotted towards Parnold's car which was poised at the exit of the track. When he reached the car Parnold was leaning on his elbow with his face out of the side window with a questioning look on his face. Campbell pointed to the lane running away from the road through the poplars opposite Parnold's car. 'Frederick Twilling didn't walk along the main road. He walked through the lanes. The murderer could even have picked him up from down there and brought him here,' said Campbell. Catherine Fenman wouldn't have seen a thing from where she was parked. He wanted to say to them about his stupidity at not seeing such an obvious possibility, but he didn't. He bit his lower lip instead and asked Parnold for the map of the area.

He glanced at Jenner next to Parnold and wondered briefly at her frown. Hadn't she pointed out the lane before? He wasn't sure. Having brought himself back to the map, he traced the path with his finger in an inverted "L" shape across the crisp paper. As he suspected it came out on the road that ran down from Jonathan Twilling's gate-house. Asking Parnold to pick him up from the other end of the track he set out to walk down it.

He glanced at his watch as he crossed the road. He was feeling peckish and guessed the others were too, but he was not going to stop now.

The track was muddy from tractors, trailers and sugar beat harvesters churning the field and dragging soil onto the path. Campbell picked his way through in semi darkness. The mist was patchy, one moment making the air in front of him seem almost solid, the next disappearing leaving the air thin, chill and clear. He checked his watch again. Its luminous numbers and hands told him it was eight p.m. He was making good time. The shadow of a building formed in front of him. Its semi-circular silhouette suggested a dome until he searched his mind for some local shape to match it. He realised it was an old Nissan hut. The path turned sharply right as it passed this building. He carried on to the road where a blue gate stood open. He walked through expecting to see Parnold's car. There was nothing there. It was now completely dark.

He sighed. They must have decided to go and get something to eat, he thought. He felt his stomach twinge with want and he started to trot towards the main road to keep from feeling hungry. It hadn't taken him quite as long through the lanes as it had to walk on the main roads. It was five minutes shorter by this route. Campbell concluded that Frederick Twilling would have had more time to meet someone if he'd walked this way.

At the junction with the main road he saw a car pulled over onto the verge with its headlights on. The mist was thin under the warmth of the trees. He felt more comfortable as he went towards it. He was ready to tell Parnold that he was waiting for him in the wrong place. A few paces on he saw that it wasn't Parnold's car, but a white car similar to the Fenman's.

He peered inside. A man lay slumped over the steering wheel with his fluffy white hair obscuring his face. He opened the car door. The courtesy light lit the scene. The man's arm nearest the door hung limply from its shoulder. He felt the man's hand. It was cold and lifeless. He felt for a pulse at the man's neck. He found none. White pills caught the light. They were spilled over the body's lap, odd ones had lodged in the grooves of the olive green corduroy gardening trousers.

He felt down around the body's feet. On the square of hard rubber he felt the smooth curves of a pill bottle.

Suddenly everything was thrown into shadow.

Powerful headlights dazzled Campbell from behind the white car. He squinted in the general direction of the light source and called, 'Parnold, we need assistance. It looks as though someone's had some sort of an attack and died in their car.'

The car's headlights remained on full beam as the driver's side door opened and a figure came towards him. Parnold was always hustling and sharp. Campbell rarely felt inclined to move rapidly, his gentle trotting pace was saved for emergencies and thinly spaced rushes of enthusiasm. He urged Parnold to turn down his headlights. His Scottish lilt straining across the distance between them. Instead Parnold returned to his car and brought it level next to him.

'What's going on?' asked Parnold from his car window.

'Dead body in the car; seems like natural causes.' Campbell précised the events of the past few minutes to get the situation moving as quickly as possible. 'And where have you been?' He allowed himself to swear under his breath.

'The chip shop,' confessed WPC Jenner. 'We were starving. We thought it would take you longer than it obviously did to walk around those tracks. And it took longer than we thought to get the chips.'

'So Donald Mercer tells me,' countered Campbell. 'Parnold, get the usuals for this other poor man.'

'We did get some chips for you,' said Jenner offering Campbell a creamy paper parcel which was effusing greasy aromas that made Campbell's mouth water.

'Thank you,' he said taking it.

'Sit here,' said Jenner hopping out of the passenger seat. 'I'll just have a look at our heart attack.'

Campbell made himself comfortable in Jenner's vacated seat and ate his fish and chips. By the time he'd finished the body had been removed and he was mulling over in his mind who Reede could have been working for prior to Jonathan Twilling when he was interrupted by Jenner's exuberant voice.

'Do you know who the dead man was?' she asked brandishing the brown pill bottle, with the name of the patient printed on it.

'Who?' asked Campbell in a tone of genuine enquiry.

'George Robinson. The friend of Catherine Fenman's mother, you know, Doctor Bane. Doctor Bane and George Robinson lived together,' said WPC Jenner as if she were passing on gossip.

'Don't let anyone touch George Robinson's car until I get back,' said Campbell apparently ignoring Jenner and screwing up his chip paper carefully into a tight ball and tucking it under his passenger seat. 'I've been thinking, the way to find this murderer is not only by looking at the opportunity or characters of our suspects. Anyone could have had those. This is about place. The deaths of Frederick Twilling and Kelvin Silverton occurred in a place suitable for the type of murder. A stabbing or a shooting could take place anywhere.'

'Sir?' asked Jenner.

'Mrs Twilling, formerly Mrs Petry, nee Miss Sarah Beaver is the person I need to talk to with her long family line in the butchery trade. It won't take long, so we'll be able to go and see Doctor Bane about George Robinson afterwards.'

The journey to see Sarah Twilling was short. The headlights of Parnold's car picked out the drive. Campbell compared it to the rough lane that led down to his own cottage, and preferred this one, which was in good order from frequent maintenance and little use.

Sarah's sister, Karen Henderson, came through from the back of the house to let the three of them in. Campbell heard a door open and close some distance away and her foot steps on the flag stones. Parnold went in first, then Campbell, and, lastly, Jenner.

'We've been in the kitchen, Inspector,' said Karen. 'I don't know how my sister managed to live in this place. Do you know the only company she had was a daily woman for a few hours each week? If only I'd realised how unhappy she was. He only let her out for Council meetings.'

By the time she'd finished speaking she was opening the kitchen door. The warm air generated by the Aga was almost overpowering after being in the cold night air and the cool hall. The visitors unbuttoned their overcoats.

The room looked cosy with its scrubbed wooden table, red quarry tiled floor, cream walls and emerald gloss painted wood trims. A large dresser displayed a range of colourful plates, and the kitchen chairs had cushions tied to them in a variety of dainty flower prints. The bottom half of the windows were covered with ivory coloured lace. It was a woman's room, thought Campbell, as the room with the floral curtains and settee, where he had first interviewed Mrs Twilling, had been. This woman could assert her taste in her own home. Whether it was because Frederick Twilling hadn't cared or whether she had a strength of character that could have matched her husband's underneath her delicate exterior, he didn't know. But now he had to gamble.

'Mrs Twilling,' he said, 'I have to ask you some more questions.' She sat on one of the cushioned wooden chairs against the table and folded her hands in her lap. WPC Jenner also took a seat while Parnold stood by the door. Campbell took his place opposite Sarah Twilling with the width of the table between them. 'Tell me about Michael Reede.' he said.

'How did you know?' Sarah Twilling asked.

'This room told me. You are a survivor Mrs Twilling,' said Campbell. He took a moment to enjoy the surprised expressions on the faces of his colleagues.

Then Mrs Twilling spoke. 'I hired a private investigator.' She sighed. 'I should have said something when Frederick died, but I felt so responsible. Michael Reede was so irritating – a bit like a salesman. He would say, "Stay lucky". It was very annoying.' She paused. 'I felt his investigations might have triggered the murder. But Frederick had hurt me so terribly, not physically. He had never hit me. But his shouting was awful and he would throw the furniture about. It made me nervous. I wasn't sure what he would do next. I wanted to leave and he wouldn't let me. If I'd phoned the Fraud Squad or something I would soon have been shown to be guilty in some way, so I employed Reede.' She looked at her hands on her lap.

'Did you know he was on leave from the detective agency?' asked Campbell. 'He was doing the work for you without his office knowing.'

'He did ask me to pay him cash, and that suited me.' Sarah Twilling looked at the plates on the dresser. 'Frederick let me buy anything I wanted.' Katherine Henderson had been standing by the sink, now she came over and sat next to her sister.

'From the internet,' said Karen.

Sarah Twilling gave a resentful twitch, turned to Campbell and half smiled. 'Even Reede couldn't resist a quick buck.' Saying it in her prim English way, the Americanism seemed out of place. 'I wanted him to get evidence against Frederick, something I could use to destroy him which wouldn't destroy me.'

Parnold moved forward, 'Did you have your husband, Frederick Twilling, murdered?' he asked.

'No, Officer. You can see I'm not capable of murder. I could not take a human life or arrange for one to be taken. I was scared that night he died, when he went out for that walk. Frederick looked so angry. I thought that he had found out about Reede.'

'You seem very calm, Mrs Twilling,' said Parnold.

'I am, Officer. Whatever happens now, my mental torture by that man is over. I shall grieve for him. I have no choice, but when it is over, I will be free. Two men have tried to destroy me. It will not happen again.'

'Thank you, Mrs Twilling for being open with us,' said Campbell. 'But we need to know more about your family history. At the moment you are looking guilty. Fear of reprisals from your husband for hiring Reede seems a reasonable enough motive for killing him and Reede would certainly have found out about your involvement with the planning applications. He might have passed that information on.'

'Not now he's been bought out by Jonathan,' scoffed Sarah.

Campbell agreed but said nothing. He also agreed with her that she was not the type to have carried out the murders but he had to get the information and this seemed like the best device to do so. 'If you enlighten us on this it may help us move on and away from you as a suspect.'

'Really, I don't understand the connection.' Sarah Twilling sighed heavily. 'I worked for my father Ernest Beaver at his Hillvill shop. I met my first husband there.'

'Hillvill? I'm sorry, Mrs Twilling, I thought you told me your husband's shop, 'Petry's' was in Ouse Crossing?' queried Campbell surprising himself at his interruption.

'It was. My first husband had two shops one at Ouse Crossing and one at Hillvill – but not to start with. My family home was at Hillvill. I was brought up there. My father had a shop at the side of the house. Frederick was a Saturday boy there when I was a little girl. He was an attractive teenager. It must have been those memories of him that made me marry him when Harold died.'

'Mrs Twilling, do you mean Frederick Twilling used to work for your father?' asked Campbell. Mrs Twilling nodded. 'Please continue,' he added.

'When my father passed away we sold up his house there and moved to Ouse Crossing. My husband bought another shop at Hillvill in London Road.'

'Where was the slaughterhouse?'

'We had a new one built at Ouse Crossing, before my husband lost his money, but my father's had been at the back of his shop.'

'What became of these slaughterhouses, Mrs Twilling?' asked Campbell. 'It is important.'

'The one in Ouse Crossing was pulled down to improve a bad corner. I don't know what happened to Father's. It was no good to anybody it was too small, more like a large garden shed than anything.'

'Where was it?' asked Parnold.

'I thought you'd know, you sound local, but perhaps too young,' she said to Parnold. 'It's on Tonne Road, next to the Bane's house. Evelyn Bane's father and mine were great friends. Evelyn's a bit older than me. I can remember her bringing the new born baby Catherine home. Looking back on it, she was little more than a girl herself. Evelyn's mother had died years before and her father died in a stubble fire when Catherine was small. He left her well provided for, but she hated that child. She wouldn't have even given the baby a name if her father hadn't called her Catherine. Poor man. She left Catherine with nannies, and she had many different ones. You could hear the rows Evelyn had with those girls all the time. Then she sent the child to boarding school. She was really too young to go. I don't think she was eight when she went.'

Campbell, Parnold and WPC Jenner buttoned their coats and moved towards the door. Campbell said, 'We will be passing on some of these matters, Mrs Twilling, so do not think this is the end of it. However, we must take our leave of you. Thank you for your help.'

As they reached the car Campbell noted there was barely any mist on this higher ground but he wondered what it would be like towards Hillvill.

'I wonder what Mercer would say if he knew Reede was originally hired by Sarah Twilling,' said Jenner.

'Aye,' said Campbell thoughtfully. 'Parnold, Hillvill.'
'Yes, Sir.'

# Chapter 18

Catherine was steered by Evelyn across the neighbour's yard. The older woman swung the beam of her torch over a square brick building. A faded sign Catherine hadn't seen before told of a long gone family business, 'Beaver's the Butchers'. Catherine's memory of this building was of it being a shed. The family which had just left and the one before that had used it for garden tools and deck chairs, as had all the people she'd ever known there ever since old Mr Beaver had died when she was about eight or nine. Even then he'd used it to keep the lawnmower in.

The memories jerked through her head mixed with efforts to make some sense out of her mother. 'What are you doing?' she asked.

Evelyn said nothing but opened the door. The place had been cleared for the sale. The most recent owners had left several weeks ago to live and work elsewhere. Evelyn turned on the light. This room was more than just empty and clean; it had been scrubbed and refitted. The white tiles were crazed from age but there was the smell of paint, acrid and new. The light bounced off the walls and ceiling dazzling Catherine for a moment. Then she saw two huge metal hooks hanging down from the ceiling on chains. Over a concrete channel were more chains with pulleys attached waiting to heave weights up from the floor and two carousels of slightly smaller hooks hung like chandeliers. The drain, thought Catherine, expected the flow of life that would come from the dead weight that would hang above it. This equipment was new and shining. She realised that Evelyn had murdered Frederick Twilling and Kelvin Silverton. Evelyn's lips trembled in a proud smile. Catherine wanted to panic, but she had too much at stake.

'Isn't it splendid?' Evelyn asked.

Catherine couldn't answer.

'I used to come over here as a girl and watch them.' Evelyn paused to admire her handiwork before adding, 'I would have liked to have been a butcher.'

'Evelyn, you're not well,' Catherine soothed.

'What a lie. I'm a doctor, aren't I? I would know if I wasn't well. You were always a lying child.'

'I was lonely. You ignored me.'

'I didn't want you,' said Evelyn.

'You made that clear enough.' She said it as pleasantly as she could while she scanned the room. 'Where are the girls, my daughters, your grandchildren?'

'Hush, all will be well. They are safe.' Her mother patted her on the arm condescendingly.

Catherine's self-control was not enough. Anger edged into her voice. 'I want to see them now.'

'I don't think so, Catherine. I don't think so,' said Evelyn. Catherine felt a needle stab into the arm her mother was holding close to her. 'You'll sleep now dear, don't fight it,' said the woman above her. It was the well-practiced manner of a doctor. Any belief that this woman was ever her mother left her just before her consciousness was taken away.

The mist was thinning under the trees by the time Campbell reached the place where George Robinson had died. The breakdown truck was backing towards the white car with its orange beacon swirling into the damp air.

"It shouldn't be doing that," thought Campbell, so he asked Parnold to pull over.

'Why?' complained Parnold. 'We should be going straight to Beaver's old place.'

Campbell shook his head, he wasn't going to explain. He just muttered, 'I left instructions for George Robinson's car to be left alone. I should have looked at it before.'

Parnold swore softly as he slowed the vehicle. Campbell heard, but ignored him.

As they came to a halt, he opened the door, without haste, and walked over to George Robinson's car calling and signalling to the break down truck driver to stop. The policeman who was giving backing instructions to the driver realised what was required and copied his superior's gestures and shouts.

'What was wrong with this car, Constable?' asked Campbell.

'Out of petrol, Sir,' said the policeman. 'Not the time to get an attack on a lonely road like this one,' he observed. Campbell noticed him glance towards his colleague stationed a few metres up the way to warn the very occasional car of the obstruction. It was WPC Garden.

Campbell leaned into the now empty car and pulled the hand-brake, which was already on, as hard as he could. He took a torch from the traffic policeman and went round the back of the vehicle. He lay on the ground next to it and eased himself underneath. The granular surface of the road prickled against his back as he touched the underside of the car. Dust fell down onto his face.

'It's in a fair condition,' he informed the gathering of feet collecting by the car. 'My wife couldn't wait for me to fix her car, she went to the garage,' he added conversationally.

Parnold muttered sarcastically, 'We really needed to know that. While you're under there someone else could be being murdered.'

'Petrol has a lingering smell,' reported Campbell. 'You can always tell if it's leaking.' There was a moment's silence. 'Here it is, a hole in the petrol tank,' continued Campbell. 'There was one in the Fenman's car. To make a car stop in the right place you would have to put just the right amount of petrol into the tank just before its journey and the hole would have to be just the right size. Even so a lot would be down to chance.'

Campbell was helped to his feet by Parnold's outstretched hand.

'It's obvious,' said Parnold, 'that the Fenmans are the murderers and that they are hiding out at Beaver's old slaughter house, next to Catherine Fenman's mother, Dr Bane. God knows who the two of them are going to bump off next. We should be getting over there instead of dawdling here.'

'You're wrong and you're right,' said Campbell. 'I agree that we must get there quickly as I fear Catherine Fenman is in danger.'

'Alright then, she could be in danger, but only from her husband,' said Parnold. 'You have to see that he is the murderer.'

Campbell could see Parnold was getting angry from frustration so he decided to keep him busy. 'Car,' he said as a direction to him and Jenner that it was time to continue their journey to the slaughterhouse. He called to Garden to join them.

As they set off, Jenner swore under her breath. 'Sir, Catherine Fenman's children are with their grandmother, Dr Bane. There's been a twice daily check there to see if Catherine Fenman has turned up. The officers who called said she hadn't, but they thought she might come back to see her children. They saw them reading in the living room. Could they be in danger, Sir?'

'It's a risk, Jenner.'

Parnold thumped the steering wheel with the heels of his hands and pressed the accelerator to the floor of the car.

Campbell lifted the radio and arranged for other police to be available for back-up. He didn't want them to approach the slaughter house until he arrived as such action could be critical for any member of the Fenman family. With the speed they were travelling at, and the mist thinning, they would arrive in only a few minutes.


The first thing Catherine heard when she awoke was her mother saying that Molly and Laura were safe.

'Where are they?' Catherine asked.

'In the house,' came the bored reply from Evelyn. 'I'm not interested in them.'

Catherine wondered how long she'd been unconscious. Slowly she remembered what had happened to her and as her awareness increased she felt a new sensation. It pulsed fear through her system. She was encircled by lengths of blue rope and her hands were tied behind the back of the kitchen chair which she found herself sitting on. This was stationed underneath one of the carousels of hooks. Catherine ducked instinctively as the hooks swung close to her eye-line.

Evelyn was wearing a heavy plastic apron, wellingtons and a blood stained boiler suite. 'Hearts, lungs and livers from the animals would hang on there. Of course, I had to buy in the ironmongery. The ones that were here originally had long gone,' she said.

Catherine saw the pride which her mother felt for this place and these things and wondered if Evelyn intended to use them. She realised the maternal ability to read the thoughts of offspring was still working when Evelyn said,

'I like it in here. I hadn't meant to use it. I wanted it to be a museum piece.'

It made her mother more dangerous. She had to try to mask her fear, turn it into anger. She had turned the misery of her childhood into strength, now she had to turn this situation around.

Evelyn had started talking again. 'I practiced on the dog.'

'Kimber?' Catherine was numbed by her mother's callous brutality.

But her mother's thoughts had already moved on. 'I met Fred by the old Nissan hut about the time you ran out of petrol. I'd phoned him and told him I would make a claim against him. Money, that brought him running. It was easy. I'd set up a gantry earlier and...' Her mind seemed to dwell on her actions until she said, 'I intended to kill you with Frederick Twilling that night, but your husband turned up. I didn't have enough dope for him as well. I got away just in time. Then I thought I could increase your torture before I killed you. I could kill your friends and loved ones, let you find their bodies. I wanted you to feel the torment you gave me.'

'Frederick Twilling was nothing to me. Why kill him?'

Evelyn ignored her. 'When I went to kill Robert, I found Kelvin Silverton creeping around your back gate. They were talking to each other. I drugged them both. It was so easy. I killed Kelvin. There wasn't really room in your shed for Robert.' She sounded teasing.

'Robert? Where is he? What have you done to him?'

'Don't be melodramatic. You always were as a girl. I thought before you died you'd like to know what I've been doing to you, that I am the one who has manufactured your misery. I wanted you to know that.'

'Where's George?' asked Catherine. 'I saw him go?'

'I sent him away. He won't last long.'

'Why?'

'I changed his pills,' snapped Evelyn.

Evelyn pursed her lips and picked up a knife with a yellow plastic handle and a six inch curved blade. 'I was even after Sadie Groom. A man calling himself Reede saw me. He said I couldn't disturb her, she was sleeping.' She started to sharpen the knife, testing the blade by shaving the hairs on her arm. 'I left them. A waste of my efforts. She would never be loyal to you. I could see that. And her bloke! What a complete moron! I left them to make their own misery.'

'When was that? She didn't say anything.'

'A couple of days before you brought the children over. I don't suppose her lover told her. He was just leaving.' Evelyn paused. 'You were in such a rush that day...'

Catherine shuddered at her mother's murderous intent. She shook her head. None of this was helping. 'I'm your daughter. Mothers care for their daughters. They don't kill them.' Catherine used her feelings for her own children and tried to project them on to her mother. But as she said it she knew she sounded unconvinced.

'That's why I've done all this. I wasted my money and time on you. Haven't you worked anything out?'

Catherine had never wanted to examine her mother's motives. Now this madness made it impossible to work out the truth. The knife reflected the light. She needed to keep her talking. Play her mother's game, so she asked, 'Why try and kill poor Sadie?'

'Because you went to her with your troubles. Without her you would have crumbled.'

'Do you hate me that much?' asked Catherine.

'You were the poison in my life, the cancer that ate at me.' Evelyn glared. Her teeth were clenched and her chin was vibrating.

'I don't see that. You ignored me, kept me away. You went on to study to be a doctor. I just lived here, when I wasn't away at school. Why didn't you have me adopted?'

'Your grandfather wouldn't let me,' said Evelyn pouting.

'He died.'

'I was a doctor. Doctors don't do that sort of thing.' Evelyn held her head on one side. Like a child choosing sweets, thought Catherine. 'You haven't worked anything out, have you?' taunted Evelyn again. 'You don't even know who Frederick Twilling was. Have you no curiosity?'

'He was a land developer,' suggested Catherine, to keep her mother's game going and the knife half forgotten.

'He was your father,' corrected Evelyn. 'We were teenagers. He was a Saturday boy at the butchers here. He had such energy. I loved him so much. I thought he would love me and our baby. Instead, when he found out I was pregnant, he brought me in here. It was empty being a weekend. And he hung me upside down.' She pointed at the pulley. 'He held me by my hair and threatened me with a knife against my throat. I had seen what they did in here. To him I was an animal. He said I was never to tell anyone that you were his child. I would have to pay in every way, but you couldn't taint his life.' Evelyn paused. She was breathing heavily.

'Why now, Evelyn? This has been going on all my life. It's too late to take out your hate on me.'

'I could tolerate his first rejection. I could do things for him. When he put his first wife away in an institution, I helped him. I knew he would come back to me eventually…' Evelyn's voice tailed off for a moment. 'Then he married that Sarah Beaver, Petry – whatever her name was. She'd lived next door to me as a child. The butcher's daughter. She was a bit younger than me. I couldn't believe it. I started to arrange Frederick Twilling's execution in the manner he had threatened mine. Then I decided you had given me all the pain you were going to. You were to die with him.' Evelyn looked at the knife.

Catherine reacted at the same time as her mother to a groan coming from a metal enclosure. While Catherine felt her body quiver with fright, Evelyn moved over to the source of the noise.

'This is where the cattle were stood to be anaesthetised before death. The slaughter man would use a stun gun. I haven't been able to get one of those,' she said. 'It was only after I killed Frederick that I started to plan your new exit and decided to use my little museum here.'

The solid metal rattled from being kicked on the other side. Evelyn smiled and turned a lever that made the side of the enclosure slide upwards. A human animal fell out into the drainage channel. It was tied hand and foot and its mouth was gagged. Evelyn wrapped blue rope around its legs and heaved it up on the pulley.

It was Robert swinging from the rope. Catherine could see his face. She screamed his name and strained at her bonds. The anguish she felt for her husband blanked out any other thoughts. His eyes were open. He blinked them hard as if clearing his vision. Behind the strip of plaster he was making angry yells. He twisted his body until he rocked and swayed. Evelyn laughed at him.

# Chapter 19

Catherine realised she was the only one who could help Robert. 'Evelyn, listen to me,' she said. 'You must have already captured Robert when I spoke to you on the phone the morning he disappeared.'

'I didn't lie to you,' said Evelyn. 'I didn't say he wasn't here.' Evelyn didn't look distracted from her task.

Catherine persisted, 'You always thought him worthless, so why waste your time on him now? Look at me. I am the creature you hate. Kill me not him.' Somehow her bonds had loosened, a hand was free. 'Slaughter me instead.'

'Sheep die willingly, where do you think the saying, "Like a lamb to the slaughter," comes from? There is no pleasure in that for me. I want you to be like a pig and squeal. Squeal, I told you to squeal.'

Catherine's ruse seemed to have worked. Evelyn was moving away from Robert and towards her.

The only sound Catherine could make was a hollow snort. Evelyn shook her head. Catherine tried again. This time the sound was porcine. She could see that the steeled edge of the knife was grey from sharpening. The older woman pulled up Catherine's sleeve and shaved the hairs off her daughter's arm. It was Catherine's free hand. She'd kept it in place while her mother shaved it, but as soon as the knife moved away she grabbed the hand that was holding it.

The strength of her grip matched the furious strength of the older woman. They fought. Catherine was dragged with her chair across the slaughter house by Evelyn. Her mother shoved the chandelier of hooks away. The two women had moved before the hooks swung back and past their original position to continue to arc back and forth across the space.

Before it settled again the combatants were close to Robert.

Catherine hadn't wanted to hurt her mother when she'd first grabbed the knife, just restrain her, but the years of betrayal and hate with this final madness had turned her into the animal her mother thought she was. She would not only fight for her life and that of her husband's with the same ferocity as Evelyn was using to take their lives from them, but, if she had the opportunity, she would kill her.

By rocking, Robert made himself swing. He knocked into Evelyn. Her grip must have loosened: she dropped the knife. Catherine found it in her own hand. She wanted to cut her mother's throat. She sliced the remaining bonds securing her to the chair with the knife and approached the older woman.

'It's over. At last,' said Evelyn. 'I knew you would be the cause of my death.' All her ferocity seemed to have left her. She knelt down and lifted her chin to expose her neck, laying her palms on her lap.

Even though she wanted to, she could not kill her mother. And now she had to respond to her fear for her daughters. Catherine went around Evelyn in a wide circle to free Robert from his bonds. She glanced at the mad woman, who was still in the same position. Catherine was shaking. 'We have to find the children,' she whispered hoarsely to her husband, not wanting to draw her mother out of her trance. But she couldn't manage the pulley chain one handed so she put the knife down. The chain clattered as it ran down letting Robert, still tied, rest on the concrete floor.

'That was the mistake Frederick Twilling made, Catherine. He thought I was harmless,' said Evelyn.

She turned and saw Evelyn, the knife back in her mother's hand.


'The door's bolted from the inside,' observed Campbell. He shrugged his shoulders slightly. 'Parnold, break it down.'

In instant reply, Parnold thrust his square shoulder to the old slaughterhouse door. Under new paint, the perished wood cracked and holed under the pressure. He pulled away a broken plank from around the lock, pushed his hand through and slid open the bolt. The door sagged on its weak hinges as it was wrenched open to reveal Dr Bane poised with her back facing the door and a knife in her raised hand. Even the noise from the door being broken open had not caused Evelyn Bane to turn. Campbell announced that they were the police.

'Are the children in here?' he asked.

Evelyn Bane paused. Without moving she said, 'They're in the house. They are irrelevant.'

'Garden, go look for the children.' Campbell heard Garden go but did not stop his concentrated observation of Evelyn Bane.

Parnold went to take Evelyn down but Campbell stopped him. She was too close to her intended victims. If she heard him move she could easily kill Catherine or Robert.

He thought for a moment. His officers would have to move together. He nodded to Parnold. The arrangement was set up with a gesture towards Catherine and Robert Fenman, cornered by walls, steel and hooks. As Campbell pounced on Evelyn, Parnold and Jenner made for the Fenmans, police stab-vested bodies shielding the intended victims, but only partially protecting the policemen from Evelyn Bane's knife.

Campbell caught Evelyn's knife hand and twisted it behind her back until she dropped the weapon. He felt Parnold and Jenner on either side ready to take Dr Bane down. But instead Parnold went for the weapon on the floor. Dr Bane lashed back into Parnold's shin. Campbell's grip loosened and Jenner had yet to get a grip on the prisoner. Evelyn Bane bit into Campbell's hand and kicked the knife away across the slaughterhouse floor. Campbell clung onto her as long as he could.

'Get the Fenmans out of here, Jenner,' he directed. 'Parnold, leave the knife.'

But it was too late, Doctor Bane pushed back with all her force breaking her own arm as she jammed Campbell against the wall. She retrieved the knife with her good arm and crouched with it on the far side of the room. She swished it backwards and forwards menacingly.

'The burning of the fields of stubble, once the wheat was harvested used to be the custom,' said Evelyn Bane. 'The fire cleanses the crop, so the farmers tell us. But I've seen spirals of black smoke reaching into the sky, charred black dust falling like rain everywhere. It's filthy.'

'Why do you mention that now?' asked Campbell.

'Because that is the first time I tried to get rid of that thing.' Dr Bane gestured towards her daughter. 'I put her in a field of straw that was being burnt. But my father saw me from the house and came and fetched her out of the field. I tried to stop him. But I couldn't. He saved that wretch.' Evelyn stuttered, 'And, died of his burns.'

She was beyond listening, Campbell was sure of that, though he knew he must try. He opened his mouth, but before he could speak Dr Bane threw herself onto the carousel of hooks. The metal spikes caught in her eyes, fatally penetrated her brain and her neck. The one in her neck found the artery and her heart pumped her blood out onto the floor, where it found its way into the drain. Campbell turned to check on Mrs Fenman and found that Jenner had already shielded her from the view. Mr Fenman was staring in horror. Campbell went over to stand between him and Dr Bane as he tried to lift her from the hooks and compress the wound. He felt her body shake for the last time as her life left her. He put her down carefully on the floor and looked up. The slaughterhouse was empty.

By the time Campbell stood outside with the Fenmans the lights of an ambulance were swirling into the yard through the mist. The shadow of Garden and two small human shapes coming out of a nearby shed were picked out by them. The policewoman explained that the children weren't in the house because she'd heard them calling from one of the outhouses. They'd been locked in, but seemed only cold and shaken. Campbell sent them in the direction of the ambulance to be reunited with their parents, and turned back to Parnold and Jenner.

'We have to be open to all the possibilities. Evelyn Bane's attitude to her son-in-law was important, and she did not tell the truth about any misappropriated drugs. She could have stored them for some time. Catherine and Robert Fenman turned out to be the victims. Evelyn Bane was warned by our visits. She had already killed Frederick Twilling and Kelvin Silverton. She knew she would soon be discovered.'

'But why?' asked Jenner.

Campbell, rotated his wrist and rubbed at it. 'Other than she hated her daughter? The Fenmans will tell their story later. But I know how Dr Bane set the murders up. You noticed that Dr Bane, George Robinson and the Fenmans all have the same make and model of car. They even have the same size engine. They are just different colours. Dr Bane planned for her daughter to find Frederick Twilling. She planted a capsule of eucalyptus in the heating system of the car which gradually filled the interior with fumes. Her daughter is highly allergic to eucalyptus. Dr Bane had even changed the amount of petrol in the car and holed the tank. She would have fixed the windows too, but they were already jammed.'

'You're just guessing?' queried Jenner. Parnold was silent.

'George Robinson's car told me,' said Campbell, 'that she had tried it out on his first. She was lucky, Catherine's car stopped just where she wanted it to. But, perhaps, she would have enticed her across the forest to the site wherever the car ran out of petrol. She wanted to frighten and confuse her daughter.' Campbell watched his toes curl upwards. 'Dr Bane followed Catherine homewards and met Frederick Twilling down the lane. He would never have agreed to go to her home and, of course George might have been there. To make Catherine panic and to delay her, she'd removed the torch, petrol can and spare tyre from the boot of the car. She even used the tow rope to hang her victims up.'

Campbell looked at Catherine and Robert and wished them well in his head. His job was done and his own hearth and home beckoned.

Bruised and bitten, he remarked to Parnold that his wrist felt better for the exercise.

Parnold asked, 'Pardon me, Sir?' He paused. 'The pathologist has arrived.'


Catherine clung to Robert in the ambulance, and she was relieved that he held her in the same way. Molly and Laura were snuggled against their parents asleep.

Had she really been the daughter of a mother who had hated her? That was what Evelyn had told her in that madness of the killing house. Sometimes she'd thought their dislike for each other had been because of her own adolescent jostlings to escape her childhood, and these had not stopped when she became an adult. Sometimes she'd thought she was guilty of some wrong doing, something she could have helped, but her wrong doing had been in being born. And that was not down to her. She wanted to believe there had been love between them, if hidden, before the cruelty of Frederick Twilling had finally manipulated Evelyn into complete insanity and her own destruction.

Evelyn had taken so many people with her. Yet, Catherine felt the guilt rested with Frederick Twilling. She could never call him her father. There was a sudden and complete emptiness inside her and she shivered.

Looking at her family she wanted the past to disappear. But she knew it wouldn't, only fade. She remembered the suffocation of the allergy attack in the car the night of Frederick Twilling's murder. The memory of smoke choking her – a connection to her mother's attempt to murder her which had resulted in her grandfather's death. She hugged her children tighter. 'They aren't allowed to burn straw anymore,' she said out loud. 'It's been banned,' and she was pleased. She had the feeling that they were all walking out of a pall of smoke together, and once their eyes had stopped smarting and they had coughed and choked up the filth in their lungs, they would continue.

Campbell looked out over the fens swallowed by night and became disconnected with the present events. He found himself thinking of Scotland, and events from a former time. He dismissed them even before he could visualise them. The past was a scary place. You didn't have to stay there. Castle Campbell had nothing to do with him or his bad memories. That fairy idyll with its autumn fire colours was just a place to go and remark that some remote ancestor might have had some connection with the place. Margaret's persuasive leaflet dropping would not change his mind. You can leave the past any time you like and you don't have to go back. He would not be setting one foot in Scotland this year. His memories would remain undisturbed and that was the way he liked it.

The End

## ABOUT THE AUTHOR

Pamela St Abbs lived in Norfolk for most of her life. She now lives in Scotland with her husband. She also writes as Mary Bale when writing about her eleventh century detectives, Abbess Eleanor and Therese, Abbess Eleanor's protégé.

www.ingramcontent.com/pod-product-compliance
Lightning Source LLC
Chambersburg PA
CBHW070332130626

46556CB00007B/2818